SUGAR DADDY SANTA

K LEIGH

Sugar Daddy Santa Copyright 2022 by K Leigh

All rights reserved. No part of this publication may be reproduced, distributed, or transmitted in any form or by any means, including photocopying, recording, or other electronic or mechanical methods, without the prior written permission of the publisher, except in the case of brief quotations embodied in critical reviews and certain other noncommercial uses permitted by copyright law.

Cover by Daisy Allen

Edited by Amanda Cuff at Word of Advice Editing Services

Proofread by Malynda Schlegel at Proofreading by Malynda

Formatted by L.S. Pullen at Indie Author Book Services

DEDICATION

*Dedicating this one to myself.
To Kayleigh,
Thank you for writing something that gave you so much joy
when you needed it most.*

Sebastian

PROLOGUE
CHRISTMAS EVE

The chill in the air isn't all that has me shivering as I navigate the snowy roads home. I got held up at work, which is nothing unusual, but aggravating when you have something else on your mind.

Finally, I extracted myself from my duties as CEO of Sterling Enterprises and made my way from the bright lights of D.C. to my estate on the outskirts of the city, and as the engine shudders to a halt, my skin prickles in anticipation. My beautiful fiancée is waiting for me, and she doesn't know I've taken the rest of the year off so we can elope.

My jet is fueled up at the airport, awaiting her wishes. She spent the month of December planning the Christmas gala my company throws annually, so the break will be good for us both.

My house manager, Phoebe, left a few days ago to spend the holidays with her family, so Charlotte and I will have the house to ourselves. Maybe we can celebrate for a while before we head to the airport.

The thought of burying myself inside her, of her crying out my name, euphoric with our plans, spurs me faster up the front steps. My fingers shake as I punch in the security code, and I knock the snow off my shoes against the porch before slipping inside, closing the door as quietly as possible.

The tree in the foyer illuminates the otherwise dark entrance, all of Charlotte's childhood ornaments adorning the beast. I came home from work a few weeks ago to find her struggling to get it into the house. It took the gardener, me, and Charlotte to manage, but she was pleased with the results.

My keys clink against the wood as I toss them and my wallet onto the entryway table and slip out of my shoes before putting them neatly underneath.

Carefully maneuvering around the wet tracks my shoes left, I make my way through the first floor, where there's no sign of my fiancée. The gas fireplace is still on, so she's here. She would never leave the fire on if she were heading out somewhere.

I take the spiral staircase two steps at a time, then come to a stop at the landing of the second floor. The third floor is practically empty, although we'll turn it into a nursery and playroom when the time comes. My chest puffs with pride at the thought of holding my future children.

A movement interrupts my thoughts, a soft shuffling followed by a murmur of voices. Maybe she's on the phone with her mother. They talk a million times a day. I push against my bedroom door, unable to stop the smile from spreading across my face as I announce my presence.

"Honey, I'm home."

The shrill shriek that follows pierces my eardrums. The scrambling of two bodies as they attempt to cover themselves in sheets and random articles of clothing are too much for me to comprehend. Why would she be naked in our bed with another man? But my mind computes the facts after a moment, my heart shattering into a billion pieces.

Charlotte's eyes well up when I finally get the nerve to look her way. The gardener attempts to abandon ship, his feet still tangled in the sheet on the floor. He finally escapes, brushing by me. The tree in the corner of the bedroom illuminates the room.

His footsteps down the stairs echo around me as my knees hit the floor, the lights from the tree with my tears.

ONE

Sebastian

FUCKING CINNAMON

One Year Later

Fucking cinnamon. Why does every manufacturing company seem to think the only scent acceptable during the holidays is cinnamon? Those damn scented brooms are scattered throughout What A Room, the home decor store that just moved into my mall.

If they hadn't paid two years in advance, I'd demand they throw them away. My investors wouldn't be happy with that, so I clench my jaw and make my way up the aisle, holding my breath for as long as possible. I'll need a damn allergy pill when I get out of here.

Which will hopefully be soon.

"Hey there, welcome to What A Room." The chirpy greeting startles me from somewhere behind me, and I spin around to find the origin of the piercing noise. I know I'm not exaggerating its shrillness, because "Jingle Bell Rock" blares throughout the store, and I heard it clear as day over that.

A noise between disbelief and disgust escapes from between my lips before I can contain it at the figure before me.

She's dressed from head to toe in bright red and green, tinkling bells dangling from her elf hat and skirt. My gaze lands on her shoes last, and sure as hell, they curl up like the shit the Whos wear. Between the cinnamon, the music, and this ensemble before me, I want nothing more than to escape up the mall and head back to Sterling Enterprises.

"Are you alright, sir?" The voice is lower now, and I raise my eyes to find a pair of warm golden ones watching me with concern.

"I'm fine. Why wouldn't I be?"

"You look pale," she remarks. "Would you like to sit down?"

"No, no. I'm here for a meeting. I'm Sebastian Sterling." I raise my wrist to check the name I typed into my watch earlier, but the elf's glittery name tag catches my eye, and suddenly, I have no issue remembering it... because it's right there in sparkly gold letters.

Amber the elf is the person I'm meeting with.

Of fucking course she is.

"Oh, Mr. Sterling." Her smile doesn't waver the whole time she's speaking. "You're earlier than I expected. If you'll follow me, we can meet in the office."

She darts around me, and I follow her through the brooms until we turn at the end of the aisle, her damn shoes jingling all the way. She halts quickly, and I nearly fall into a display in my hurry to keep from crashing into her. A customer meanders by, stopping in front of us to peruse a shelf.

"In my experience, it's better to be early than rushing."

She throws a smile over her shoulder, and she's so close I can make out green specks among her brown pupils. "You gotta live a little, Mr. S."

Now that I'm really looking at Amber without focusing on

her ensemble, I see that she's beautiful. Not in that supermodel perfection way like most women I know, but in a comforting way. Her face lights up without a lot of makeup. Her mouth is naturally full and pink.

We're so close, her scent swarms around me, momentarily stronger than the cinnamon—sweet, citrusy... oranges. The customer passes by, and we're on the move again. When we reach the office door, she turns the handle, motioning for me to go in before her.

I refuse. Never in my life have I let a woman hold the door open for me, and I'm not going to let it happen now.

"Have a seat. I have to grab my tablet from my purse." She skips away, and I close my eyes for a moment, resisting the urge to bang my head on the wall.

The office isn't decorated at all. It's bare and boring, and I feel right at home as I settle into one of the armchairs. My body relaxes into the soft, plush fleece fabric. Being away from all the stimulations in the mall for even just a moment has already calmed my nerves.

The door opens and Amber slips inside before locking it behind her.

She walks daintily, as if the floor is made of glass. After a moment, I realize she's trying to not jingle the bells on her shoes.

She collapses into her desk chair with a loud sigh. "Man, I'm tired."

"I'm sure you are. Retail is difficult enough. The holidays just multiply it."

Something brushes against my leg, sending an electric shock through me. I open my mouth, but no sound comes out. Something keeps me from moving away from the warmth, the comfort of her foot against my leg.

"I'm so sorry." The warm feeling disappears immediately,

replaced by a coldness I hadn't noticed before. "I just need to stretch a minute. It's been brutal."

We stare at each other, and it hits me that she's waiting for me to speak. Of course she is. I'm the one that asked for the meeting.

Painting a smile onto my face for good measure, I cut to the chase. "As you know, Charlotte is no longer overseeing the Christmas event Sterling Enterprises hosts every year."

Amber's fist tightens on the desk, her smile faltering a bit. "Yes, I was informed. Thankfully, I was able to find this job on short notice."

The concept of struggling, of financial hardship, is foreign to me, so I'm not sure how to respond to her comment. It's an obvious remark, but I can't commiserate, and she's surely aware of that. Moving forward seems to be the safest option.

"I'm now in charge of making sure this event happens successfully, and I'm hoping you can be persuaded to come back."

Amber sighs, and it's not a happy one. It's a resigned sigh. It's an *I'm about to let this guy down* sigh. I've heard them before.

"Mr. Sterling—"

"Call me Sebastian, please."

"Sebastian." My name sounds musical in her voice. "We put a lot of work in for Ms. Fletcher over the past few months, and she just abandoned the whole thing. Every caterer the company hired backed out because of her. They let a lot of us go, including me. Now it's less than a month away. I doubt there's anyone in the state with availability at this short notice. I don't know what else can be done."

"I completely understand that, I do." I don't want to beg, but maybe I can bribe. Gathering all the politeness I possess, I force my mouth into what I hope is a more genuine smile. It feels foreign on my lips.

"I need your help, Amber. Please."

Amber

Sebastian Sterling needs my help. It's laughable. My qualifications aren't super impressive. I'm rounding the bend to thirty years old and spend my days playing in decorations for whatever holiday is next. I'm an okay party planner, half-decent part-time retail employee. I am one hell of a dog mom, though.

He shifts in his chair, clearing his throat again. I'd offer him a peppermint, but the way he eyed my outfit earlier has me second-guessing myself. Pure disgust was written all over his face, so he'd probably want to wash the candy off. He probably thinks he's better than me because he's rich and well-known.

Coming to me for help was probably a blow to his pride, but knowing that Charlotte caused this mess tugs at my heartstrings. She was a terror to work with. I've always done my best to be amicable, but she was the toughest I've ever worked with.

"I don't know that I'd have the time. I'm working a lot of hours here right now." *To make up for the money I lost because of Charlotte.* No need to regale him with my financial woes, but it's the truth.

"Babs seemed to think they'd be able to cover for you." He leans forward, resting his elbows on his knees and clasping his hands. It's like he's praying. It ruffles my feathers that he spoke to my boss about this. "You'd have a job waiting for you after the holidays. I'll pay you the rest of what Charlotte owes you and a hundred thousand dollars on top of that. And you can do whatever you want. Order and decorate to your heart's desire. Doesn't have to be what she planned." His wide eyes focus on mine with a gleam of determination I wouldn't have thought possible five minutes ago when we met. "I want the gala to be absolutely perfect. No expense will be spared."

My mind froze back at the extra money mentioned. A hundred grand. It would take me years to make that much money. I could pay off my car. Hell, I could buy a *new* car.

Not yet prepared to answer either way, I glance down at my tablet. Staring back at me is a photo of me and my parents. My dad was holding me up on my first Christmas. I was six months old, and they were helping me hang my first ornament. My mouth is split into a toothless smile, my eyes wide and illuminated by the Christmas lights on the tree.

I've loved the holidays for as long as I can remember, literally, and this picture is proof.

"I'll do it," I finally answer, pushing aside my personal thoughts. Christmas without my dad has never been the same, but this isn't the time or place to get emotional about it.

He would want me to take the job, to use the money for something good. Something important. I open a new document on my tablet, preparing to take notes. "What's your email? I'll send you links to all the files so you can see what I'm planning or spending."

"Unnecessary. I don't care about any of it." He shifts in his seat to pull out his wallet. His hands distract me as he flips through his cards, his fingers expertly moving at warp speed in a way that makes my breathing quicken.

"Here." He slides something across the desk. When he moves his hand, the shiny black credit card reflects the light above us.

"I'll deposit your money into the account Ms. Fletcher had on file, but use this for any expenses for the event. Including your food, gas, and your outfit for the night of the party. Order whatever you see fit. And here's my business card."

I take the thick cardstock from him.

"My cell is there," he continues. "On the back is the address for the estate we're having the party at. My house manager, Phoebe, is there twenty-four seven. You can call her anytime and go by."

I pull out my phone and punch in his number. "I sent you a text with my name, so you'll have my phone number too. When is the best time to tour the house?"

Now I'm the one clearing my throat. This didn't seem real till he gave me a credit card. Now it's becoming too real too fast, and if I wasn't already sitting down, I think I'd be dizzy.

"I'm never there." He's visibly relaxed since I said yes. He's not friendly per se, but he's not as grumpy looking as before. "I have a place here in the city."

He pushes the chair back and rises to his feet in one fluid movement. He buttons his suit jacket, but not before his dress shirt tightens against a well-defined chest and abdomen. His hands loop the button easily, his deft fingers then moving up to straighten his tie.

Oh my god.

In the midst of the gala talk and his awkwardness in the store, I was oblivious, but upon closer inspection, it's obvious this man is sexy as hell.

Oh, fucking shit.

Looking down to collect myself, I grab his credit card and

flip it over. In shiny black letters is his name. Now I truly am dizzy.

Planning a billionaire's gala for the rich and ogling his body.

What kind of Christmas have I gotten myself into?

TWO

Sebastian

THE HAPPIEST SEASON, MY ASS

"For god's sake, Herschel, it's being taken care of." Despite each curve my driver takes, the whiskey bottle in my hand never wavers as I make myself an Old Fashioned.

"It better be, Bash. Or I'll take my money elsewhere next year." Herschel is my company's biggest investor and my ex-fiancée's father, but he's known me since I was in diapers.

People rarely call me Bash anymore, but he's slipped more than once during a board meeting. Normally, he's on my ass on the daily. But January ends our fiscal year, so I can count on a phone call two or three times a day in December.

The happiest season, my ass.

"I don't mean to be so hard on ya, kid." His guttural chuckle worries me. The hacking cough that follows fills the car through the speakers.

"Have you been smoking again, Pops?" The old man may be an ass, but he's been like a father to me since my own passed away. Whatever happened with his daughter, I still care about him.

"Just one or two, Bash. Don't get uppity."

"Pops..."

"What did I say, kid?" he warns.

"Fine, fine." I throw my hands into the air, forgetting he can't see me. "The gala will be perfect."

"You've never planned that shit before. Charlotte always did. What makes you think you can start now?"

"I'm not planning it, Pops." My chest twinges at her name, but I shake off the pain.

"Who then? The house manager?"

He's the nosiest old fucker I've ever met, but damn if I don't want to make him proud. "I've met someone." Not a lie. "She's helping me out." Also true.

"Oh, Bash," he exclaims. His passionate response has me afraid he'll choke again. "That's wonderful! I've been hoping you'd find someone. Can't wait to meet her. You guys will have to come to brunch soon."

Ah, shit. I should have seen that coming.

"I'll let you know, Pops. Gotta go. I have a call coming in." I've dug my grave deep enough.

"Bye, kid."

The line disconnects and I down my drink, the liquid warming my throat and chest.

I need it for where I'm about to go. The estate. I've avoided this place like the plague since the breakup, but I have to come to the gala, and before that happens, before Charlotte sets foot into my house again, it can't look like she still lives there. My loneliness can't linger in these halls any longer.

I take a deep breath as the car comes to a stop. "I'll call when I'm done, Mike."

"You got it, boss." Mike tips his hat and I climb out, giving my former home a long look after shutting the door behind me. Mike continues around the circle and down the road.

The front walk was paved a few weeks ago in preparation for the gala.

"Mr. Sterling." Phoebe throws open the front door as I walk up the steps.

I hired her when I took over the estate and company after my father's death three years ago. She's managed the house ever since. It has to be kept up to a certain standard, and I've never been patient enough to deal with the details.

I would have paid her extra for the gala itself, but she'll be taking the next two weeks off to spend the holidays with her family. She'd give it up if I asked, but there's no way I'd ever suggest it.

"Hey, Phoebe. How are you?" I take her hand and give it a squeeze.

"I'm doing well. Was surprised to get your call."

She turns to walk down the entry hall, but I still haven't stepped inside. The thing people neglect to mention about breakups is the ache. Sure, the person is gone, but a part of the relationship still lives inside you, scar tissue of a lost love.

"Glad we'll still be able to get the gala up and going this year."

Through the entry hall is a sitting room, where white sheets cover the furniture. Thankfully, most of it was here before Charlotte. But her paintings still line the walls, and the curtains she picked out are partially open to let the evening sun in.

"Me too. Did you meet Amber?"

"I didn't." Phoebe shoots me a wane smile. "Ms. Fletcher hadn't brought any of the planning committee here yet."

Disdain drips from her words. Charlotte wasn't unkind to my staff until I called off our engagement, but then she left messes everywhere and was just rude. Phoebe will love my next request more than anyone.

"Let's change up the place, shall we?"

"Decide what you wanna do, and we'll take care of it." She waves her hand around, and I'm sure the staff is on their toes awaiting orders.

"Everything she chose..."

"Yes?"

"Get rid of it. Donate it, of course. But rip it all out."

Like she ripped out my heart.

"Of course, Mr. Sterling." She pulls out her phone and begins typing away. "I'll alert the staff." She pauses, her fingers hovering over the screen, and when our eyes meet, I know what she's going to ask me.

"I'll take care of the attic. Leave it be."

"We'll get to work right away. Anything else?"

"That should do it. Thank you." My gratitude is sincere. This is a huge step, and while my staff is here for the money, I like to think Phoebe is more than my employee. She's part of my family. "I'll be in touch. And I'm sure Amber will be touring the house sometime soon. I've given her your information."

"I'll be in touch."

I turn on my heel, heading out of the house as fast as my feet will carry me. I ache to leave behind my heartbreak. I like to pretend it's not there. That I'm invincible. That Charlotte didn't hurt me.

But when I see our house and remember the sight of another man in our bed, it all comes flooding back to me.

Maybe the change of scenery will help. I don't even miss her anymore. It's just the idea that something about me wasn't enough.

As I get into the car, Mike glances at me in the rearview mirror and I nod. "Let's head home for the night, please."

"Sure thing, Mr. Sterling." For the first few weeks after I

moved out, it threw him for a loop, me calling the penthouse home. The estate has been home my whole life and I do miss it.

But I'm not ready to live there again. I don't know that I ever will be.

Amber

I've spent the past three nights making new plans for Sebastian's Christmas Eve gala. Most of what Ms. Fletcher wanted was stuffy. Boring. I'm adding my own twists she would have never approved of.

Today, I'm going to tour the estate. Everything is falling into place, and with the help of unlimited funds, I can get anything I want in time. My only concern is the availability of a caterer this close to the holidays. The party is less than three weeks away. Anyone Charlotte hasn't scared off is booked. But thankfully, I have a solution, and she'll be coming through my front door any moment.

I know that because my tiny yorkie is shaking from head to toe with excitement.

"Gizmo. Calm down, buddy." I scratch his ears reassuringly. He whines, rubbing his head against my hand for more pets.

The door bursts open, the knob banging the wall so hard my shelves shake.

"There's my boy." My mom bends to her knees, catching Gizmo in her arms. He laps at her face, and she turns her head so he doesn't get her mouth. "Did you miss me? I know you did."

She stands up with him cuddled against her chest and holds an arm out to me.

"I can't imagine what it'll be like when I have kids, Mom. I'll be last in line," I joke, giving her a hug.

"Oh, don't be silly." She pulls out of my grasp and smiles. "Now, let's get this party started. What's first?"

"The only issue I'm running into is catering. No one's available this short of notice." I don't fill my mom in on the dramatic details.

"I'm sure they're not. Who leaves something like this to the last minute?" Mom looks at me over her glasses with her mean eyes. "That's downright awful to even think about."

We've lived in D.C. for over a decade, but my mom's northeast Tennessee roots are ingrained in her for eternity. My granny would roll over in her grave at the rudeness.

"Yes, ma'am," I agree, knowing anything more is futile. "So I was thinking…"

"That I could cook the food." After she finishes my sentence, a smile pulls at the corners of her mouth. Gizmo yips in response, always putting his two cents in.

"You're the best cook I know. And you've made a huge dinner for our family reunion every year in Tennessee." I widen my eyes at her.

"Oh, flattery will get you nowhere, Amber. I just have a soft heart. I need to see the kitchen." To Gizmo's horror, she sets him on the couch. He begins shaking again.

"Go on now, Gizmo," I scold him. "She'll get you again when we get back."

"Oh, he can go with us." She moves to his basket of belongings and grabs his leash. He normally runs from me if I try to leash him but stands stock-still for my mom. Traitor.

I grab my purse and coat from the hook by my door, and we parade out, Gizmo in the lead.

My apartment is about thirty minutes from Sebastian's estate, but traffic adds some time to our drive. It's after ten when we finally arrive, and the whole place is surreal. It's more like we're arriving at Buckingham Palace. Mom pulls around the circle in front of the house, the brakes squealing as she comes to a stop.

"We need to get that checked," she comments as we clamber out of my beat-up beauty.

"Yes, ma'am," I agree again. We both stop short on the front walk, marveling over the house—no, mansion—before us. It seems to be three stories high, has a million windows, and there's a balcony on the second floor. It's a magnificent house and beautifully kept, but something about it seems so empty.

I haven't been here before now because Charlotte kept putting off the tour.

Gizmo takes the first steps, as if to say, "It's cold, ladies. Let's go," and we follow him to the front door. My finger hovers over the doorbell for a moment. I could still change my mind, give Sebastian his card back and go back to What A Room and work my normal hours. But the thrill of planning, the holiday cheer in the air... It's intoxicating, and I'm drunk on Christmas spirit.

After a fleeting moment, I press the cool metal surface, stepping back as the bell thunders throughout the house.

The door opens and a petite older lady pokes her head out with a smile. "You must be Amber. I'm Phoebe. We spoke on the phone." She steps back, and Gizmo leads the way in. "Oh, what a cutie." She pats him on the head.

"He's well-trained." Pretty much a lie as far as behavior, but he won't use the bathroom in the house.

"He's fine," she reassures me.

"And this is my mom." I motion toward her.

"Hi, Mom," Phoebe jokes and we all laugh, some of the awkwardness fading.

"You can call me Joy, if you'd rather," Mom jokes back. "I'm apparently the caterer."

"Well, let me show you the kitchen then, and Amber can look around the rest of the house. How's that?"

"Perfect. Will you be alright, sweetheart?"

"I'll be fine. Gizmo can keep me company."

Mom nods and follows Phoebe out of the foyer, and I'm grateful to be alone for a moment. The whole place is clean and tidy, and if I'm not mistaken, by the scent, I'd say it's freshly painted. The furniture is pristine and expensive. The walls are pretty bare, but we can no doubt find something festive to adorn them. I can picture several things from What A Room that would fit the bill.

Of course, I'm not going in the direction of a normal Christmas gala. A hoity-toity one, as my dad would have said. No, I think it needs the comforting touch of a normal holiday. Rather than the perfection of designer decorations, the black-and-white trees Charlotte had requested, I'm looking forward to taking a different route.

As I make my way through the rooms, I take notes on my notepad, labeling them for whatever room I'm in. The house is humongous, with two sitting rooms, the kitchen, a formal dining room, a ballroom, two bathrooms, and I haven't even been inside the kitchen yet. And that's just the first floor.

I complete my circle, skipping the kitchen for now to make my way up the spiral staircase. The air seems heavier as I reach the landing to the second floor, a musty scent more present here, and I make my way down the hall, peeking into each room.

There are three bedrooms, all the beds made with matching

duvets but the last and biggest bedroom is completely empty, without even furniture. It's hollow and empty, a sadness lingering amongst the cobwebs. I shut the door carefully, not wanting to disturb whatever haunts the room.

The room across the hallway is the last one on the second floor, and when I step inside, I gasp audibly. It's filled with Christmas decorations. Trees with ornaments still adorning them, stacks of wrapped boxes, signs and wreaths and mistletoe. It's a sight, for sure, and part of me wonders why they'd decorate with boring shit when they had this right upstairs.

Just as I'm about to head to the third floor, my ass starts vibrating, startling Gizmo and I both. I'd forgotten he was following me, and when I stopped, I grazed his toe. I fumble to pull my phone out of my back pocket. The number isn't saved but seems familiar, although I can't place why.

"Hello?"

"Amber." Sebastian rumbles my name, his voice warmer than I thought possible that day in my office.

"Mr. Sterling."

"Sebastian," he reminds me. He's more than polite, almost nice. My suspicions are on high alert. "Or Bash, if you prefer."

Bash is a bit too personal, in my opinion. "Okay, Sebastian. I'm actually at the house now. The caterer is here to look at the kitchen." I don't tell him that it's also my mom. I mean, she is a caterer. So what if she's not a professional.

"I'm actually calling to ask you to have coffee with me."

"Coffee?"

"Yes. Or tea. Or whatever you prefer, of course."

When I glance up, I see my reflection in the window, and my face accurately portrays my horror. What happened to him not wanting to be involved? I have very few details prepared to share with him yet.

"Very well," I agree reluctantly.

"Fantastic. I'll be there in five minutes. Phoebe will have a tray ready for us."

"Right now?" I squeak, my random scribbles of ideas hurtling through my mind like a runaway train. I'm nowhere near ready for a meeting about this.

"Why not now?"

Unable to come up with an argument, I clear my throat, collecting myself. "Alright, sounds great."

He hangs up, and I stare at my phone before looking down at the furball on my foot. He tilts his ears at me. "Right? What the hell, Gizmo?"

THREE

Sebastian

WHAT A BUNCH OF DICKS

"Thank you, Phoebe."

"You betcha." She winks at me as she sets the tea tray down. I give her a pointed look, and she scurries back to the kitchen with Amber's mom.

When I texted her to prepare a tea tray for us, she replied with heart emojis and stars. She's convinced this is truly romantic, and that couldn't be further from the truth. Amber does look beautiful today. She's ditched the elf costume for leggings and a sweater dress. She even left the damn bells at home, thank God. But the last thing on my mind is another relationship.

She busies herself preparing her tea, and I do the same, glancing at her every now and then. She bites her lower lip when concentrating on pouring the water into her cup.

"So." She adds sugar with a small plop, and the spoon clanks as she stirs. "I suppose you want details about the party. The caterer—"

"Your mom," I interrupt. I know the woman isn't a professional caterer. The way she interacted with the "caterer" was suspicious from the moment I walked into the house, and then Amber slipped up and called her Mom.

"Yes, well..."

"I'm going to be blunt with you, Ms. Crawford. Maybe I wasn't clear enough in our first meeting. I don't give a shit about this party."

Her mouth drops open. "Then why are we doing all this?"

"My investors expect an elaborate party every year. My biggest investor has been threatening to move his funds elsewhere. This is the final straw, my last chance. If he pulls out, I'll have to close several of my operations. Including the mall where your store is."

"What a bunch of dicks." She scowls at me, eyebrows furrowed. "I love Christmas. It's my favorite part of the year. But they sound like little kids. Plan my party or I'm playing with someone else."

I burst out laughing, a harsh sound at first. I can't remember the last time I laughed, so I imagine my body is as shocked as I am. Amber's smile widens, her eyes locked on mine as I wind down to a chuckle.

"They're big babies. That's all there is to it," I agree before sipping my tea. "As for loving Christmas, I... It's not my favorite."

"I noticed you're not a fan."

"How could you tell?"

"The first time you saw me, I thought you were going to throw up." Amber contorts her face into a grimace. "This is what you looked like."

My laughter is more natural this time, but I regain my composure. It's time to get down to the reason I asked her to meet with me, to get this over with.

"So, I have another favor to ask of you. And I'll double your money." On the way here, the words whirled around in my mind in a million different arrangements, but none of them sounded right. I'm just going to throw it out there.

"What's the favor?" Her wary eyes satisfy me. She's not agreeing easily, which is refreshing. At the offer of double the money, a lot of people might have agreed right away.

"My biggest investor is my ex's father."

"Oh."

"Yeah, but he's also my mentor, and I care about what he thinks." I wince at the words as I say them. I've been more vulnerable in three days with Amber than with anyone else in my adult life. "And he's under the impression that you're helping me throw this party."

"I am helping you throw this party."

"Yes, but… he thinks we're… co-hosts." I stumble over my words, dreading the fact that I may have to flat out say it.

Amber watches me silently, eyebrows furrowed together.

"He thinks we're together. Dating," I blurt out. "And we're hosting as a couple."

"A couple?" Her laugh fills the room and then cuts off abruptly. She covers her mouth with one hand. "I didn't mean that as an insult, just—"

"No offense taken." I nod, pushing my saucer back. "He caught me off guard, as well. And I can bite the bullet and tell him the truth. I just… I hate the idea of disappointing him more than he already is."

He introduced me to Charlotte in hopes I'd eventually take over his family business. It feels as if I've let him down enough. "So, would you act as my girlfriend for the next two weeks? Go to brunch with Herschel tomorrow, a few dinners, the gala. We can break up around New Year's."

Amber doesn't say a word. She just stares at me, her eyes drilling holes into mine. I sip my tea slowly, hoping my nerves aren't showing. The world sees me as this stoic, invincible billionaire, but behind the fancy suits and money, I'm just a man, and once again, I'm asking this woman for help. With bated breath, I await her response.

Amber

Despite the differences in our lives, something in Sebastian's face is vulnerable, awaiting rejection, and my heart melts for him. Like chocolate chips when you're making homemade fudge. My family is full of huggers, and my first instinct is to wrap my arms around him. I'm sure he wouldn't appreciate that. I would like to help him, but the thought of the deception, taking more money, doesn't sit right with me, either.

"Why don't we tour the grounds, and I'll think about it?" I offer, gathering my dishes carefully on the tray. "I want to decorate the exterior. Maybe you can give me some insight."

He squints at me as he adds his own cup to the tray. "You have to think about it?"

"Well, yeah. It seems... wrong to deceive people like that. I don't like lying." Moving to my feet, I glance around for Gizmo. "Gizmo, where are you buddy?" I call.

"What about the money?" Sebastian follows me as I make my way through the house to the back door I spotted in my search earlier.

"The money? Well, of course I can use the money, but my

morality is more important than any amount you could pay me."

This seems to have stumped him, as he leans against the door and crosses his arms. His eyebrows furrow, and when I drop to the floor and sit cross-legged, they move even closer together.

"What in the hell are you doing?"

"Gizmo is hiding, but if I pretend to be asleep, he likes to wake me up."

"Who the hell is Gizmo?"

"Shh, I'm sleeping," I whisper before closing my eyes and feigning sleep. A few seconds later, the soft click of his toenails on the hardwood floor echoes, and the next thing I know, a furry warmth catapults itself into my chest with a growl.

"You got me." I hop to my feet, moving my head to the side to accept puppy kisses. "This is Gizmo."

Sebastian and Gizmo stare at each other, neither of them blinking, and unsurprisingly, Gizmo cracks first, leaning forward to sniff Sebastian's offered hand. He's nosy and a sucker for pets and scratches.

He nudges Sebastian's hand until Sebastian scratches behind his ears for a moment.

"Alright, shall we?" Sebastian clears his throat, his hand dropping to his side, and he opens the back door. The cold burst of air takes my breath away, and Gizmo jumps from my arms and runs before coming to a halt across the room. "I guess he's not coming with us."

"I don't blame him." Sebastian buttons his coat as we step out onto the back deck, and I wrap mine tighter around me.

"How big are the grounds, anyway?"

"Oh, it'll take us a while to tour. Probably an hour."

An hour? Shit. I wasn't expecting that long. I just wanted to stall on my decision.

The sidewalk from the deck out into the garden still has a few patches of snow, so I watch my step as I make my way through. "Everything out here can be decorated with lights and ornaments." My fingers trail the empty branches. "We can make it look like a real winter wonderland. It'll be beautiful."

"I couldn't care less what you decide to do out here." Sebastian huffs, leaning against the post of the back deck. "I don't give a shit about any of it. Just do whatever you think will make everyone happy. That's your job, right? A party planner?"

My bark of laughter surprises us both, and as I knock my shoes on the step before coming back onto the deck, I decide it's time Sebastian knows the truth. Knows what he's getting into by hiring me.

"I was a party planner for the company Charlotte hired," I begin, rubbing my hands together for friction. "But they let me go when Charlotte canceled on them."

"So, you weren't the owner?"

"I was not. Just an apprentice. I plan to start my own company, though," I hurry to explain. "I know what I'm doing. I just didn't get a fair chance with your fia—ex."

His face grows brighter and brighter, the shades of red threatening and foreboding.

I close my eyes, waiting for him to explode. Everyone does after they hear my resume. I've only worked entry-level jobs at minimum wage and never have enough experience. It was supposed to be different this time, but apparently not. I've had so many jobs not work out since I moved here that I'm usually expecting the other shoe to drop.

"Did Charlotte know this?"

"Know what?"

"That you weren't the head of the company?"

"She did. She requested someone newer, with less experience."

"Fuck." Sebastian clenches his fists, a vein in his forehead practically popping out. "She wanted the whole event to fail."

While I can't agree, I also can't disagree, because I'm not sure. So I just remain silent for a moment before slipping back into the house, leaving Sebastian to cool off.

FOUR

Amber

PICK YOUR POISON

After hours of details, dress fittings, and dragging my mom and Phoebe out of the meat department at the grocery store, I'm relieved to be home in my bed, with Gizmo curled up at the top of my head. We dropped him off before our shopping adventure, and he wasn't pleased that he didn't get all the pets he was promised, so I'm making it up to him now while we watch *Buffy the Vampire Slayer*.

My text notification goes off and Gizmo growls. He knows that means a pause in petting.

It's from Sebastian.

S: Any further thoughts on my proposal?

Fuck. After our talk outside, I gathered my mom and Phoebe, and we went out to get a few things done. Of course the thought was lingering in the back of my mind that I had yet to make a decision. The man is like the Grinch. Sure, he's not selfish, but he takes no joy in the holidays. If he would just open his eyes, have a little fun...

Suddenly, I know how I can be okay with the deception.

Me: I'll do it on one condition.

S: Name it.

Me: For every event I attend as your girlfriend, you have to participate in a holiday activity with me.

The typing bubble appears and disappears several times.

S: If you don't mind, text me your address and I'll pick you up around ten in the morning.

I hurry and send my address. As an afterthought, I send a follow-up.

Me: Just text when you get here and I'll come out. My roommate is off tomorrow and will sleep in.

I also don't need my nosy neighbors spying from their peephole. I haven't officially dated in a year, but I had a friend with benefits for a few months, and Peggy next door couldn't get close enough to him.

His next message makes me laugh.

S: I imagine Phoebe was beside herself with all of the excitement.

Me: Oh my god. Her and my mom are now BFFs. So there's that.

S: Lol.

Did Sebastian really laugh out loud, or is this one of those situations where he didn't know what to say so he filled in the conversation? Shaking my head, I copy and paste the link for the google doc I made earlier with a list of our Christmas activities.

Gizmo's hum vibrates my head, a gentle reminder that he wants to watch Buffy. After I grab the remote and press play, he falls silent again.

Me: Which one do you want to do after brunch?

S: Can I decide and tell you tomorrow? Hard to pick my poison.

Me: Sure.

S: What are you doing?

Me: Watching Buffy with Gizmo.

S: The show or the movie?

Me: Show. **It's Gizmo's fave.**

I snap a selfie of us, and I swear Gizmo almost smiles.

S: He looks thrilled.

The next message that comes through is an image. I open it to find a selfie of Sebastian, his hair no longer perfectly in place, and he's wearing glasses. He must wear contacts, then. Damn, the glasses flatter his already handsome face. Reminding myself to focus, I take in the rest of the picture. A huge fluffy white feline is curled up under Sebastian's neck, posing for the camera, as well.

S: This is Willow.

Me: YOU WATCH BUFFY.

S: Only the show. Did you find a dress?

Me: I did. Thanks, sugar papa.

Oh my god. I pressed send without thinking. Between petting Gizmo, the messages, and eyeing Spike and Buffy tearing down a house, my mind wasn't focused.

The phone vibrates as I shut it off without waiting for a response. I've already said it now. My mom always told me I'm good at putting the cart before the horse, and she's absolutely right.

When we moved to D.C., I was fresh out of high school, and Mom wanted a change after my dad had passed, and I was fine with that. Northeast Tennessee was too small for my big dreams. I worked random retail and food jobs while getting my party planning certifications, then went on to college for a bachelor's in business.

After graduation, I wanted to start my own business, but without the proper credit, due to my horrible spending habits and weakness for the finer things in life, I couldn't get approved for a loan. No way was I asking my mom to sign for me. So I applied for the entry-level job at The Ambience, leading me to the Charlotte debacle and back to working retail to make rent. The creak of the front door interrupts my thoughts, and a glance at the clock on my nightstand tells me it's too early for Ava to be home. Hopefully, she's okay.

My roommate has been more than forgiving in my times of trouble. I've paid her back every cent, but I don't want to let her down again. She's absolutely perfect, her life is planned and budgeted, and she's an associate at a prestigious law firm now.

I slip out of bed and into my house shoes, moving quietly out of my room so as not to disturb the sleeping Gizmo. He's sprawled out like a king on his side of the bed. God forbid I ever have a real boyfriend. He'll have to sleep in a kennel.

The thought of Sebastian curled up in Gizmo's unused kennel makes me giggle, but I stifle my laughter and close the door carefully behind me. Our bedrooms are both connected to the living room, and the small kitchenette is separated from the living room by a counter. Ava's notebooks and computer are all open on the counter, and she's pacing back and forth, peering at one book, then another, then typing furiously on her laptop.

"Rough day?" I ask.

"I'm this close to proving my client is innocent," she rambles off, pushing her tight dark curls out of her eyes. "I can taste it, Amber. This whole thing is going to change the face of the music industry."

I know her client is a high-profile musician, but she can't share any other details of the case with me. And I don't think she would want to, anyway. Ava is the most straightlaced person, honest to a fault. She won't even let me sneak candy into the movie theaters.

But hey, who wants to pay five bucks for a small box of Raisinets?

"I'm so proud of you. You're just doing the damn thing." The warmth in my words is genuine, but part of me can't help but be a bit jealous. All I wanted when I came here was my dream, and I failed. That's okay, though. Sometimes you can find a new dream.

"I couldn't have done it without you. You've taken care of me all through school." She swings her arm around my shoulders, hugging me close.

"Well, to be fair, I had to feed myself too. There was a bit of an ulterior motive behind my cooking," I joke, leaning into her hug.

Shortly after we became roommates, I took over cooking. Ava does the cleaning. I'm a slob, but she has no patience for waiting on things to boil or bake, and after eating half-cooked potatoes once, I politely suggested the arrangement, which she agreed to gratefully.

"Speaking of." I clear my throat, leaning on the counter after she releases me and returns to scouring her papers. "I won't be here for breakfast."

"Oh? You worked earlier."

"I'm going to brunch with Sebastian." I cringe at the memory of our texting convo. "And I called him sugar papa earlier."

"Brunch? That's not too bad. But sugar papa?" She stops, her eyes lasering in on me again. "For real?"

"It's a long story, but cliffs notes: I'm being his fake girlfriend till this shit is over with, and we're supposed to have brunch with his biggest investor."

"Oh my god. What are you going to wear?"

"Honestly? I have no idea. I thought about my elf costume from work." Imagining Sebastian's face if I hopped into his car with my elf ensemble sends us both into fits of laughter, the sound echoing around the kitchen, and I have to hold my stomach from laughing so hard. "Oh my gosh. He would be mortified."

"Might want to leave that one at home, then." Ava wipes her eyes carefully. "We should probably decide on something, though." She sets her clipboard onto the table and heads to her bedroom. I follow suit, unsure of what I've gotten myself into.

Sebastian

After a sleepless night of tossing, turning, and overanalyzing Amber's text, it's a relief to get out of bed and prepare for the day. Brunch with Herschel won't be terrible, but convincing him that Amber and I are truly involved will be the real test. He can read me like a book.

Sugar papa. After some Googling, I discerned she was referring to a sugar daddy... and while I am paying her and taking care of her, it's not in exchange for anything inappropriate.

Hopefully, she doesn't see herself that way, as something that can be bought. I certainly don't, and the fact that it's possible I've come across that way leaves a nasty taste in my mouth. But money is how I've always solved my problems, and in hindsight, I have been throwing it at her.

Respecting Amber's wishes, I wait in the car for her to come down from her apartment. I drove myself today, and Mike was practically chomping at the bit to talk me out of it. Nosy bastard wanted to get the scoop on my new "girlfriend".

The door flies open and Amber hops in, a flurry of freezing air accompanying her.

"It's colder than a witch's tit." Amber talks through chattering teeth, slamming the door behind her.

My small chuckle surprises me. "I've laughed more since I met you than I have in a year."

"I'm glad you're entertained by my antics." She fiddles with the heat dial, then rubs her hands together in front of the vent.

I do a double take before focusing on the road to pull into traffic. "No wonder you're cold. You didn't wear any gloves. Or a coat!" Out of the corner of my eye, I see her rub her hands together, and it's all I can do not to reprimand her. It's not my job to take care of this woman, so why do I suddenly feel a flash of responsibility for her? I suppose it's because she's helping me out so much.

"I didn't even think about it." Amber waves away my concern, turning her head to glance out the window. We pass several familiar places on the way, but a few new stores have popped up since I've actually paid attention to what was available. Some names sound familiar, and there are plenty of new restaurants, as well.

It hits me then how long it's been since I went anywhere besides work and home. We ride in companionable silence, nothing uncomfortable about the space between us, and I'm relieved that this isn't awkward. It's probably the quietest I've ever seen her be, to be honest.

"So, we probably need to establish our story," she blurts out after a few more minutes.

I don't risk a glance at her with the traffic but nod in agreement. "Probably."

"First of all, how long have we been dating?" Amber shuffles in the seat, pulling her phone out of her back pocket, and begins typing furiously.

"What are you doing?"

"Taking notes. We want to get our story straight."

Damn. This isn't supposed to be that serious, is it?

"How long do you think seems plausible?" Her fingers pause, awaiting my response.

"Um, no more than a month. We don't want any pressure to be... serious. Herschel will be ringing wedding bells if we're not careful. How about two weeks?"

"I'm helping you plan a company gala after only two weeks?" Her tone is doubtful, and I rack my brain.

"Well, we could say a few months, then."

"Okay. How did we meet?" she rattles off while texting into her phone madly.

"Let's stick to the truth. I came into the store you work at while I was in the mall one day."

"Easy enough," Amber agrees. "Where are we having brunch?"

"At Herschel's penthouse." I flick my turn signal before turning into the complex and find the first empty parking spot I can. The building looms before us after we exit the car and lock up.

Tension rolls off Amber in waves, and she takes a deep breath and reaches for my hand. "Can I keep my name? Or is a fake one necessary?"

"I don't think that's—" I glance over to reassure her and find her smirking, a dangerous twinkle in her eye. "Oh, you're being sarcastic. Amber, just be yourself. That's the best way to make this go by quickly, get the whole gala over with, and go back to our normal lives."

As she collects her purse and phone, I rush around the front of the car to open her door. She steps out gracefully, and it's the first time since I picked her up that I've gotten a really good look at her. I've seen her twice before—once in her elf costume, and another in leggings and a sweater.

This version of Amber isn't quirky or comfortable. She's simply stunning. As she rises to her feet, my eyes refuse to stray from her legs. Knee-high black boots fit the curves of her legs. The hem of her dress stops midthigh. If it weren't for her leggings, she'd be showing a lot of skin. The dress is plaid, except for her long black sleeves. Our eyes meet, and her lips are trembling.

"You didn't wear a coat." I remind her.

"I won't freeze." She waves me aside, shutting the car door with me still attached to the handle.

My feet slide across the ice, but I brace myself, leaning against the car before I hit the ground.

Amber's mouth drops open in an O, and she covers her face with a gasp. "Oh my god. Are you okay?"

"Perfectly fine." I clear my throat, taking a hesitant step and then another away from the vehicle. As I slip my coat off, the cool air seeps into my shirt, the chill biting but bearable for the short distance.

I'm not letting Amber freeze, though. Ignoring her protests, I wrap it around her shoulders and button the top button to keep it closed. Appraising her expression, wide eyes and pursed lips, I remind her, "You can't plan my party if you have pneumonia. Alright. Let's go."

Amber falls into step beside me. As we make our way to the door of the condominiums in silence, all I can think about is what a bad idea this might have been. I've dragged this practical stranger into my business all for the sake of pleasing everyone else, which is what I'm accustomed to doing. But I suddenly wonder if I can pull it off.

I don't want my father's business to fail, though. He built it from the ground up and entrusted it to me. So, whatever it takes, I'll pull through. We enter the lobby, the warmth flooding my face, and a determination to get shit done filling me with new reserve.

Amber

I can't think straight. When Sebastian wrapped his coat around me, his scent invaded my senses, and as we wait for the elevator to the penthouse, it's all I can do to stop myself from pressing my nose into the fabric and inhaling deeply. Describing the way he smells is difficult. It's a warm, comforting scent that I've encountered before but can't put a name to. It's driving me crazy.

But then the elevator doors open, and we're stepping out into the foyer. I push aside my distractions, pasting what I hope is a genuine smile onto my face. I was nervous about the outfit Ava picked out, but I have to admit, it does flatter my body. My hips have always been smaller than my chest, but the pleats of this dress make me look more even. Glancing sideways at Sebastian, I'm startled to find his face is white as a ghost.

"Hey, hey." I slip my hand into his, his gloves wrapping my skin in a warm hold. "What's the deal?"

"I'm fine," he breathes out before painting on a smile. "Just a little warm in here. I'll be fine."

He doesn't look fine. I hang his jacket onto the coat rack, and after he removes his gloves, I tuck them into his coat pocket. His hands are shaking, and I take them in my own, squeezing firmly.

"We can leave if you want. I'll say I feel bad."

He shakes his head, returning my squeeze. "I'll be okay. I feel better without the gloves." His face is returning to its normal shade, and his hands aren't trembling.

"Take a few deep breaths." I stare into his eyes, hoping to convey some reassurance. "Breathe in through your nose, out through your mouth." He obeys my directions, his breathing regulating, and just as a small smile tugs at his lips, a booming voice startles us both.

"There you are." A short, round man comes around the corner, his salt-and-pepper hair stuck out in every direction. He reminds me of an angry bird, really. His eyes flick between us, lingering on our intertwined hands. "You lovebirds can't hang out in the foyer all day. The food is getting cold. Or hot, depending on which plate we're referring to." He chortles.

Sebastian and I drop our hands, and Herschel grabs him in a one-armed hug, a humorous sight, as the old man's head barely reaches Sebastian's shoulder. "I've missed you, m'boy. It's been too long since you came for dinner."

"Long hours. You know how that is, Herschel." Sebastian returns his hug, and I'm relieved to see his face has relaxed completely now.

"Not too busy to romance this lady, though, eh?" Herschel offers me a hand, and I take it, shaking it firmly.

"That's some handshake you've got there."

"I'm Amber. Amber Crawford. And my dad always said a firm handshake is your best first impression."

"Ah, was he a businessman?"

The image of my dad with his filthy clothes and greasy face after a long day of brake testing trains pierces my mind. "No, sir. He was a mechanic for the railroad."

Herschel lets out a low whistle. "Now that's a job, Amber. I wouldn't last two hours doing something like that. You all follow me. Denise just set the table for us."

He turns and leads the way, and we follow. The table is beautiful, adorned with fresh fruit and several flavors of muffins and pastries. As I take a seat next to Sebastian, all I can think of is how my dad would have gotten this pristine white tablecloth filthy the moment he sat down. What would he think of me, taking all this money for hardly nothing?

I'd like to think he'd be proud of me for doing something I love, but it's still more than this job is technically worth. He always had a plan and achieved his goals. I'm just hopping through life, grabbing on to whatever stepping stone passes by. We begin making our plates, and I push away my thoughts, determined to make a good impression on the old man.

"So, tell me all about you, Amber." Herschel scoops eggs onto his plate as he talks, followed by portions of everything else. After an encouraging nod from Sebastian, I begin making my own plate as I talk.

"Well, I grew up in Tennessee. After my dad passed away, my mom and I moved here."

"And what do you do?"

What do I do? Shit. The man knows I'm helping throw the party but apparently doesn't realize it's also a job.

"I'm actually in event planning." I shoot Sebastian a smile, eyes widening for his approval, and he nods imperceptibly. "That's why it worked out so perfectly for Sebastian and I to host this amazing event together."

"About time something lit a fire under him." Herschel

chuckles. "I was starting to worry, especially about the food." He shovels another spoonful of food into his mouth, and silently, I hope he doesn't ask for details about our caterer. Thankfully, he moves on from the conversation.

"And how did you guys meet?"

Herschel takes a sip of coffee, eyes following us over the rim of his mug, and I prepare myself for the show... the show we're starring in.

Reaching over, I cover Sebastian's hand with mine, and after a moment, he wraps my fingers in his, his skin warm on mine.

"You're so damn nosy, Herschel," he jabs, leaning back in his chair as if he were at home. "We met when I was in the mall one day. Now, what have you been doing, old man?"

I'm suddenly envious of his comfort, the manners ingrained in me by my mother making it impossible for me to let my posture stray.

"Oh, you know, dealing with the same old shit." He sighs, leaning back, as well. "New computer programs, secretaries moving around to avoid drama." Herschel rolls his eyes. "Dumbest shit I've ever heard."

"I feel that. Secretaries are underappreciated and have very little help," I counter.

"I'm sorry. What do you mean?" He leans over the table to look closer at me.

"Just what I said. They work so hard and barely make ends meet. They could use a break."

Sebastian's eyes focus on my face as I talk, and it's all I can do not to look away. He looks at me as if I'm the brightest thing in the room, but we both know that's untrue.

"They could learn to deal with the norm. That's what they can do." Herschel snorts. "People have made comments since the beginning of time, never hurt anyone before."

My face flushes, my neck and cheeks so warm that now I may actually be the brightest thing in the room. I don't want to piss off Sebastian's client, but the words erupt from me before I can stop myself. "Maybe it did hurt people, but they were expected just to deal with it. Now people realize and value their worth, Mr. Fletcher."

Herschel and Sebastian's heads both whip toward me, Herschel's fork poised in the air. His eyes burn into me, but I don't look away, and he sets his fork down with a clink before averting his gaze to Sebastian.

"And what do you make of this, Bash?"

"I don't speak for Amber. She's her own woman. But I support and agree with her."

Herschel harrumphs, and we continue our breakfast. By the time we're heading downstairs in the elevator, the air between us has cleared some. As we step out into the bitter cold again, Sebastian clears his throat. The snowflakes fall around us in a lazy haze, melting on my sleeve as soon as they hit.

"I'm... I apologize about Herschel."

"Why? You're not the sexist ass." I hold out my hand. "Give me your keys."

He reaches into his pocket, then freezes as what I requested registers. "Why?"

"Because we have an activity to get to, and it's a surprise since you didn't pick one, so I have to drive." I flash him a grin, wiggling my fingers at him expectantly.

FIVE

Amber

MAYBE HE'S AN AXE MURDERER

"You're joking." Sebastian stares at me from the passenger seat. He's already agreed to let me drive his car, and that was difficult enough.

"I'm dead serious. You can't do Christmas shit and not listen to Christmas music on the way."

He closes his eyes as if he's being tortured, and maybe he is, but it's part of the deal. "Now, I can pick or you can pick." After connecting my phone to the car's Bluetooth, I open my music app and hand him the device. He takes it with a curious expression, glancing down at it then back at me. Has the dude never seen Spotify before?

"You can pick first," I offer, turning the ignition and shifting the car into drive.

"No, it's just..." he starts. I glance over at him, my foot still firmly on the brake. "You want me to use your phone?"

"It doesn't bite, Sebastian." I laugh at the mental image of my phone attacking Sebastian out of nowhere.

He scoffs, turning his attention back to picking songs as I focus on the road and ease out into traffic.

"So, no clues as to where we're going?" He taps the screen, choosing "Hallelujah" by Pentatonix. A personal favorite of mine, though one could argue that it's not a Christmas song. I'll let it slide this time.

"You know it's a surprise."

"I said a clue. I didn't actually ask where we're going."

He's got a point. Touché. "Okay. It's a tradition I used to do with my dad."

"Not your mom?"

"No, Mom sat this one out. She's not an outdoorsy kind of gal."

"Oh, so we'll be outside." Sebastian drawls out the *oh* theatrically, and I could kick myself for giving away such a big clue.

"You're a bit sneakier than I anticipated." The further we drive, the more space appears between the houses, until the road is lined with trees. The snow quit falling earlier, the sun now melting the winter's assault away.

"I'll get something else out of you before we're there."

"Oh no, you won't. I'm on my guard now," I tease him, keeping an eye out for our road.

Peering ahead at the street signs, I realize we listened to half the Christmas album instead of picking back and forth. Either way is fine. It's the thought that counts.

"Here's our turn." I flick the turn signal before taking the gravel road at a much lower speed than I had been traveling.

I press my tongue against the roof of my mouth, hiding my laughter as Sebastian peers out of the window in anticipation. We pull into the lot, and I park the car and lean back in the seat easily. "Here we are!"

Sebastian turns to me, his eyes wide in horror. "You wanna cut down a Christmas tree, and you didn't bring gloves or a coat?"

Well, fuck.

"Sebastian." I don't even know what to say at this point. I dragged him out here to the middle of nowhere, and I'm not even prepared.

"Luckily for you, I have a coat and gloves." Sebastian chuckles, buttoning himself up and slipping off his gloves. "I can do the chopping."

I groan, covering my face with my hands. "I feel like such an idiot."

"You shouldn't. We all fuck up sometimes," Sebastian reassures me, and after a moment, I step out of the car too. "Now, I think I have an extra jacket in the trunk." He presses the button on his key fob and emerges with a navy blue hoodie.

"I won't lie, I can't believe you own a hoodie." I slip it over my head, and the hem falls almost to my knees. We fall into step, the snow crunching under our feet as we head toward the makeshift booth.

"Hey, friends," the elderly man greets us jovially, his wrinkles multiplying as he smiles. "I'm Junior, and this is Hart's Tree Farm." He throws his arm out with a flourish.

"I'm Amber. Nice to meet you."

"Are you guys from around here?" His friendly tone is refreshing after the city, and he chats as if we've known each other forever.

"From D.C.," I reply.

"You've got a bit of an accent, though."

"Good ear." I laugh. "I moved here from Tennessee a few years ago and went to college here."

"Where'd you go to school?"

"Just the community college."

"Oh, you may know my Rachel."

"I'm sorry?"

"Rachel's my granddaughter."

Racking my brain, I can't recall a Rachel. "I'm sorry, I don't think I know her."

"Oh, Junior. You think you know everyone through someone." The woman seated beside him rolls her eyes, but they still glow with affection. "He usually does, though, to be fair. Alright, how can we help you folks?"

Sebastian glances between us, so I take the reins. "Sebastian here... He's not a fan of the holidays."

They both gasp, their eyes widening. Junior covers his heart, as if my words pain him. "Sebastian? Faye, are you hearing this?"

Faye nods solemnly, speechless in her own horror.

"I'm trying to introduce him to the best things about this season. Your adorable farm is first on our list."

"List?" Sebastian grumbles. "I hoped you'd forgotten about that."

"Yes, list." I elbow him, smiling over at Junior and his wife. "So, he's going to cut down a tree today."

Junior dives under his counter, emerging with an axe and handing it to Sebastian, who handles it as if it was made to fit his hands. Honestly, it catches me off guard. Maybe he's an axe murderer. That would be my luck: going into the woods with an axe murderer.

Shit.

"Oh, dear. You didn't bring gloves?" Faye nods toward my hands. "I have extras, hang on."

She turns on her heel and collects a bag from her chair. She digs inside, the tip of her tongue poking out of her mouth, until she emerges with a pair of crocheted mittens. She pushes them into my hands, shushing my, "But...but..." And when the soft yarn touches my skin, I cease my objections.

"Thank you, Faye."

As I slip on the gloves, Sebastian passes Junior a few bills from his wallet for the tree and picks his axe back up. He must have sat it down during our glove debacle.

"Alright, you kids have fun, but be careful. Only the trees can lose limbs today," Junior jokes.

"Do people lose limbs often?" Sebastian questions them, worry creeping into his tone.

"It's fine, Mr. Grinch. C'mon." I hook my arm through his elbow and lead him toward the patch of evergreen trees. I throw a quick thank you over my shoulder to Junior and Faye as we move.

As the cold crisp air seeps into my lungs, I'm thankful for Sebastian's hoodie and the gloves that are snug against my hands. The sky is clear, and the sun is shining brightly. It's a beautiful day, even though it's cold, and now that brunch with Herschel is over, only good things lie ahead.

"Which one are we getting?" Sebastian maneuvers out of my arm as soon as we come to a stop before dozens of perky, beautiful trees. Their scent invades my senses, refreshing and clean and reminding me of when I was young.

"You have to pick. It's going in your house, remember?" I remind him, trailing my fingers along the needles of the tree directly in front of me.

"Fuck, Amber." The aggression in his tone startles me, and I turn to watch him.

"This is ridiculous. The things I do for my stupid job." He throws the axe up on his shoulder, taking off in the snow like a dwarf heigh ho-ing to the gem mines. I cover my mouth, holding my laughter at the mental image of Sebastian whistling as he worked. Likely story. We'll be lucky if he doesn't cuss the whole time.

Stepping in his tracks, I follow him as he circles the lot, eyeing the trees myself. Sure, he can tell me which one he thinks we should choose, but I'm not actually allowing him to pick a shitty tree. No way.

Just as we're about to turn the corner of the lot, Sebastian stops abruptly, and I nearly bump into him. Regaining my balance, I follow his gaze.

The tree his eyes are set on isn't terrible, but it's a bit farther away from the others. It's on the corner of the lot, and there's something sad about the way its branches lie, as if they're aware of the distance and their difference.

It's beautiful, though. The green is brilliant and perfect, and as we step closer, the scent is clean and fresh.

"So this is the one." My hands land on my hips, eyes returning to Sebastian's profile. He nods wordlessly, moving forward and swinging the axe from his shoulder.

"This is the one," he finally replies, glancing at me over his shoulder with an uncharacteristic smile. The force of his smile knocks the wind out of me.

The difference on his face is mind-blowing, his eyes lit up in the sunshine and glinting as he turns his attention back to the task at hand. My stomach squirms, not in an uncomfortable *you better find a bathroom* way, but something else. Something I can't quite put a name to.

Shaking myself back to the present, I focus on Sebastian and on his hands curled around the wooden handle. As he swings back before bringing the axe down to the base of the tree with all of his might, I hold my breath. Then he does it again, over and over, until the tree hits the snow with a sweeping sound, and he drops the axe to the ground, his breathing now a bit heavier.

As he turns to face me, I clap my hands together. "You did it."

"Yeah, yeah." He shrugs, the illuminating smile from before

disappearing without a trace. "Now, how are we getting this sucker back to my house?"

My mouth drops open, my own lack of planning completely destroying my vision of a happy Sebastian celebrating the holidays. "Fuck."

"To be fair, I didn't think this through before we started, either, if that helps." Sebastian's eyes lock on my face, and I wonder if he can see all the thoughts I'm having. God. For a party planner, I'm shit at this activity stuff.

"Okay, my best friend drives a truck. I can call her and get her to come pick it up," I offer. "Or, we can tie it to the top of your car. *Christmas Vacation* style."

"Won't it scratch the paint?" He eyes me, crossing his arms. Is he cold, or is he doubting me?

"Maybe a bit. But hopefully not."

Sebastian shakes his head, but if I'm not mistaken, a small smile tugs at his lips. "Fine. Maybe Junior and Faye have a rope we can borrow."

"I'll go ask," I exclaim, trying to be helpful. I sprint across the snow and am halfway to the booth when a sharp pain shoots through my ankle, and I hit the snow, landing on my shoulder.

"Amber, are you okay?" Sebastian calls, the crunching of his footsteps furthering my humiliation.

I would love nothing more than to bury my face into the snow and hibernate for the winter. Do ostriches hibernate? This one's about to.

Sebastian

As I watched Amber skipping across the snow, I never expected to see her hit the ground. I drop the tree I'd been finagling and carefully take off after her, reaching her in no time. I bend down, reaching to push the hair out of her face. "You okay? Can you breathe?"

"I can breathe fine. My ego is the most wounded here." She groans, pushing herself up with her hands.

I hold out my arm and she latches onto it without hesitation. She trusts so easily. I could never. She pushes herself to her knees, and then we rise to our feet together, the snow falling off her as she maneuvers. When she leans on her right foot, her face contorts into a wince, and she groans and closes her eyes.

"I can't put any weight on this foot." She leans into my body, relaxing a bit. "I hate when this shit happens," she mumbles, and I get the impression she'd cross her arms if she could hold herself up.

"You fall into the snow often?" I quip, the sensation of her folding into my side a bit overwhelming. I don't know the last time I've been this close to anyone, really.

"No, I don't, actually." She sighs, maneuvering to attempt to walk again. She groans in pain, a low hollow sound that seems to come from her throat.

"Well, there's only one way we're getting out of here now."

"What's that—oh!"

She stops talking as soon as she's in my arms, her knees bent over one arm and her back resting on the other. Her citrusy scent invades my nostrils as I make my way back to the front of the tree lot, and it's odd how familiar it seems. How fresh compared to the perfumes most women in my daily life wear. All of them wear strong, overpowering shit. That's what Charlotte wore, too, despite me asking if she'd mind toning it down some.

Faye gasps as we approach the counter, and her eyes are locked on Amber. "Oh dear. What happened?"

"I've just twisted my ankle. It'll be alright once I rest it," Amber reassures her, pasting on a brave smile. Her face is as white as the snow. She's not tricking me.

"Nonsense, you need to have an X-ray," Faye insists. "It's better to be cautious. Let me call you an ambulance and get the paperwork."

Amber's sigh seems to echo all around us. "I'll be fine, I swear. Just need to ice it some."

"Give us a moment, would you?" I smile over at Faye, and she nods.

"Of course. Let me check on my husband."

Once she's out of earshot, I whisper in Amber's ear, "Let me take you to the ER. I'll be able to get you in and out with no issues, and then they don't have to deal with anything here." I motion toward the elderly couple.

"I really think it'll be fine with rest and ice," Amber says, not meeting my gaze.

Then something clicks in my head. She works part-time retail. I'm sure she doesn't have health insurance.

"I'll send someone for our tree," I reassure Junior and Faye as I head to my car, with Amber still in my arms.

"That's fine. We'll make sure no one grabs it," Junior says, and they wave goodbye to us. Somehow, I manage to get the passenger door open and drop Amber in carefully, although I do think her ass hits the seat harder than I mean for it to. Once I'm in the driver's seat, we head back down the mountain. Amber connects her phone to the Bluetooth again and "Carol of the Bells" seeps throughout the car.

"I'm sorry about your tree." She sighs at the end of the song, evidently ready to talk now.

"Oh, please. It'll still be beautiful." I scoff. "And it's definitely been a memorable day. I just hope your foot is okay."

"I think it's really my ankle." She winces as she stretches out her leg, and while my eyes are on the road, I can practically feel the evil glare she's shooting at her injury.

"It'll be fine. Really." I try to be reassuring, but I'm not sure how.

"It's just, next week we're supposed to do my favorite activity, and I can't do it if my foot isn't better."

I pull into Sibley Memorial Hospital just then, my curiosity piqued. "What is it you wanted to do?"

"Ice skating. It's my absolute favorite."

"Ah." I haven't seen her foot, but I know she couldn't put any weight on it. I don't know if we'll be doing any ice skating. I don't tell her that, though.

"Let me grab a wheelchair, and I'll be right back for you."

"Some date this is," she jokes. "Maybe number two will go more smoothly. I'm sorry."

I'd almost forgotten about our relationship deal, but when she mentions it, something inside me softens. She's here with a maybe broken ankle after helping me out, trying to spread her cheer, and she's apologizing. Then my heart hardens as quickly as it weakened. What does she get out of me doing holiday activities? I wish she'd just asked for more money. Then it wouldn't feel like a game.

Without another word, I jog to the emergency room entrance and grab a wheelchair, collecting myself so I'm calm once again when I return. After watching her struggle for a moment, I lift her out of the car easily and set her gently in the wheelchair.

"Thank you." She clears her throat, her eyes burning into me as I flip the foot pedals open and set her injured foot on it carefully. As we roll across the road and into the hospital, the day's events flash before my eyes. It's been ages since we were at Herschel's for brunch.

"Can I help you?" The receptionist is a heavily made-up woman with rhinestone glasses perched on her powdered nose. Her eyes flick between Amber and me, waiting on an answer.

"Yes, I think I've sprained or broken my ankle."

"ID and insurance card, please."

Amber digs into her purse and pulls out her wallet. Her fingers shake as she fumbles for her driver's license, and instinctively, I reach to help her, but she snaps it loose just as my hand grazes hers. She glances up at me, eyes wide and lips trembling, and damn if she doesn't just crawl under my skin. She breaks our gaze, sliding the card across the counter to the receptionist. Her and Amber stare at each other for another moment and she says, "And your insurance card?"

"Oh, I don't have insurance right now."

"How will you be paying?" The lady's tone changes, becoming less kind, more accusatory. She examines Amber, judging everything about her. I'm sure we look like quite the pair, frozen and tired, but she knows nothing of our financial state. My temper flares, my body warming from within at the way she's treating Amber, who I've only known a week but never witnessed being rude or unkind to anyone.

"We'll be paying cash," I interject, trailing my hand over to Amber's shoulder to squeeze her gently. She relaxes under the contact, and I'm glad she's not objecting.

"Very well. Here are some papers to fill out. There are a

few others in front of you, but we'll call you back as soon as possible." The receptionist turns away, her cheeks red, and I wheel Amber to the waiting area with a triumphant smile.

"You really don't have to do that. I have the money you paid me. I just froze up," Amber says, and I take a seat across from her. I can keep a good eye on her.

"Oh, don't be ridiculous. You're out here doing things with me. If it weren't for that, you wouldn't have been injured at all," I remind her. "It'll be fine."

"I hope so." She groans, covering her face with her hands. "I've got too much shit to do for the party, and with you."

"With me?"

"Yeah, I've made plans two or three times a week for the next two weeks." She sighs, dropping her hands into her lap. "I figure it's good publicity for you to be seen out with your girlfriend too. Herschel will probably see it online or in the paper."

"Oh, yes. Good point. That's an excellent plan."

I clear my throat, twiddling my thumbs in my lap.

"Crawford!" The nurse calls, and I hop to my feet to roll Amber back, hoping everything will turn out alright. Not just for the party, but because Amber doesn't deserve to miss out on her favorite things.

SIX

Amber

WHAT DID YOU DO TO SCROOGE MCDUCK?

"Absolutely not," I declare, sprawling out on my bed with Gizmo. Sebastian stands over me, his arms crossed and his grinch face in full force. "I'm not staying at your house."

"I'm not gonna be here to carry you up and down the stairs every time the elevator's out of order. And you'll be at the house planning and such a lot this month, anyway. Why does it matter?"

"Because this is my home, Sebastian. I'm only on foot rest for a week. It's just a sprain. I can do a lot of planning from my bed, and Ava will take care of me."

Ava watches us from the doorway, her head turning back and forth like she's watching a tennis match. I don't get fired up about a lot, but I appreciate my space. It's important to me.

"Actually...Bambi... I have to go out of town with the partners for three days."

Sebastian and I both turn toward Ava, and while his face has transformed into a glowing angelic expression, I'm throwing daggers at her.

"What did you say?"

"You know I'm trying to move up, and it's a big deal for this client."

"The mysterious client." I scoff, scooting down in my bed. "My mom can stay with me."

"She's going to be at the house practicing her dishes for the party. It's settled." Sebastian grabs my duffel bag and unzips it ceremoniously before reaching for the top drawer on my dresser.

"Wait—"

The drawer squeaks as he slides it open, and he stares down at the contents for what feels like an eternity before he pushes it shut again.

He backs away from the dresser and when our eyes meet, something clenches in my chest. I've seen him with several expressions over the past few days—frustration, anxiety, amusement. But the hot heat pouring from every inch of his body fills the room, and my own cheeks burn at the thought of him finding my vibrating friend. God.

"Right, then. Ava can help me pack," I insist, averting my eyes from his face. "I will come quietly if Gizmo can stay too."

The phrase I just used could not have been used at a more embarrassing time. Sebastian swoops out of the room without another word, and the traitorous Gizmo follows behind.

While I die of embarrassment.

"What did you do to Scrooge McDuck?" Ava whispers as she sorts through my clothes. I stare at the monstrosity they call a boot that's on my foot, wondering if I could shoot daggers through it, as well. Maybe it would disappear and my ankle would magically be healed.

"What do you mean?"

"He's like grumpy, then, all of a sudden, so happy."

"That tends to be the norm, from what I've gathered."

"So let me get this straight. You've known this man for less than a week. He's paid you all the big bucks to plan his party, be his fake girlfriend, and now to move in with him."

Glancing up from my boot, disappointed that it didn't in fact erupt into flames, I find Ava staring at me with an arched eyebrow.

"I didn't do anything to him, and I'm not moving in with him. If you're gone, he's not wrong about the stairs and the elevator. And I've got so much to do for this event." I groan, raising my hand over my eyes and reveling in the momentary darkness.

"You're for sure going?" Ava perches on the end of my bed, covering my hand with hers.

"Yeah, I'm going. It'll be fine. Christmas will be here before you know it, and Sebastian and I will go our separate ways once more."

Ava nods before continuing to sort my belongings, but my words sound hollow. When I think of them, it's different, but saying them aloud makes them seem more real. Before that happens, my grinchy fake boyfriend is going to fall in love with the holidays. I'm going to make sure of that.

"Phoebe's gone to visit her family for the holidays." Sebastian clears his throat, setting my bag next to the large bed, which looks like a cloud. I'm hanging on to my scooter for dear life, knowing the minute my head hits the pillows, I'll be out for the night. "There are a few staff around, should you need anything, and of course you can always ask me."

"So kind of you." I swallow heavily, my mind still imagining the plumpness of the pillows. At least I'm on the bottom floor. Somehow in my tour last time, I failed to find the bedroom on the lower level, but Sebastian showed me where it was, along with a handicapped accessible bathroom.

Fleetingly, I wonder why he has that, but I'm too tired to ask. "My mom will be here in the morning to work on some food details, and a florist is coming too."

"Oh, good." Sebastian nods, tucking his hands into his pockets.

It's been a long ass day. Breakfast at Herschel's feels like it was a million years ago. The silence between us isn't awkward but noticeable, and just as I open my mouth to mention heading to bed, a giant gong-like sound rings throughout the house. I nearly fall off my scooter, but Sebastian catches me easily, his arm wrapping around my shoulder as I balance my knee on my scooter again.

"Who could that be?" he murmurs, checking his watch. "It's after nine."

"Um. Nine really isn't that late. Perhaps we're old," I comment, scooting into the den behind him. When we get to the formal living room, I really don't want to sit on the pristine furniture, but I also don't want to hit the floor, so I choose the lesser of two evils and perch onto the edge of the sofa as Sebastian stalks through to the foyer. The cushions are as soft as my bed looks, and I curse the doorbell for interrupting my bedtime.

Closing my eyes, I lean back and listen to the murmur of Sebastian's voice. His words are unintelligible, but the smooth bass soothes me. Mixed with the comfiness of his sofa and my exhaustion, I'm halfway to dreamland when an obnoxiously loud screeching sound echoes from the foyer, causing Gizmo to howl from his dog bed on the floor.

I open one eye, wondering what in the world could be going on. Sebastian leads the way, dragging the top part of our tree while his driver brings up the rear with the trunk. Gizmo hops out of bed, determined to protect me from our intruder.

"Well, shit." Sebastian pants, glancing around the room. "Okay, let's prop it up here. In front of the window. At night, the lights will look great from outside."

They maneuver the branches and trunk while Gizmo dances around their feet, and by the time it's on the stand, both are sweating profusely, and Gizmo settles back in his bed.

"We can decorate it tomorrow, right?" I yawn, my vision blurry now. I took a very large, very friendly ibuprofen before the arrival of our tree, and I'm beginning to really want my bed.

"That's fine with me," Sebastian agrees. "I've still got to get back to the city and do a few things for work. I'll be here tomorrow for the food tasting, though."

A pang hits me, the realization that I'll be here without him. Sure, there'll be staff here, but it's his house and still feels a bit like I'm invading. "Alright. I'm about to head to bed, anyway."

"Let me help you get there. I'll meet you at the car, Mike."

To my surprise, he sweeps me off the couch into his arms again, his body warm and comforting against mine as he carries me to the bed. When he tucks me in under the covers, it's not as warm as being wrapped in his arms. I watch his figure as he leaves the room, the graceful quietness of his movements hypnotizing me, and when he returns with my scooter, I look away quickly.

He props it up against the nightstand and hands me a bottle of water. "I'll see you tomorrow afternoon, then?"

"Thank you again, for everything." I have thanked him a million times today, but he keeps rebuking me, saying I'm helping him more than he's helping me. I don't really think that's possible or true, but I'm in no position to argue.

"Good night, Bash." I roll onto my side, careful not to snag the ridiculous boot on the covers. His nickname slipped out but once I say it, it feels natural.

"Good night, Amber." His voice fades as I drift off to dreamland.

It seems like no time before my alarm goes off, an annoying chime that I specifically chose because it would keep me awake.

"Shut up," I mumble, swiping furiously at the snooze button. When the horrible noise stops, I pull the covers over my head, hoping to slip back into the delicious dream I'd been savoring. Clenching my eyes shut, I'm there again, tugging at the man's hair as he devours my sensitive flesh with enthusiasm. My hand trails under the covers, leaving gooseflesh along my breasts and stomach before I reach my slick heat. God, why didn't I pack my trusty sidekick?

A throwback orgasm will have to do for now. My fingers still know what to do, circling and rubbing while the image of the dark-haired man keeps at it, and just as I'm at the brink, he looks up at me with a devilish grin.

As I fall over the edge, I mutter his name in a breathless whisper. "Bash."

SEVEN

Sebastian

SHE'S GONNA CLEAN BOTH OF OUR PLOWS

I'm planning to leave the office at lunch, but it still seems like the morning drags on for years. I want to get back to the house to check on Amber—and taste what her mom has been cooking all day. Amber sent me pictures of several things, and I'm drooling by the time I lock up my office, nodding farewell to my secretary.

"See you tomorrow, Mr. Sterling."

"Have a good night, Daniele." I know I sure as hell will. We'll be sampling foods and decorating the tree. It's looking like it'll be a nice affair. My steps falter as I exit the building, it suddenly dawning on me... I'm actually excited about the holiday activities. What in the world has come over me?

"Mr. Sterling?" The clicking of Daniele's heels on the tile grows louder and louder until she stops, breathless, beside me. She hands me a Post-it note with a phone number in her neat handwriting. "Someone called from this number earlier but wouldn't give a name. They wanted to speak with you at your earliest convenience."

"Probably someone looking for a donation or something." I stuff the number into my pocket. "I'll deal with it tomorrow."

"Very well." She turns on her heel and makes her way back to her desk. She's always been an amazing secretary. My father's secretary was a bit miffed that I hired my own, but I felt it was prudent to have someone I could work well with and had a good connection with. She got over it when I doubled her retirement.

It's odd for Daniele to not get someone's name, though.

I tap my fingers on the steering wheel, humming along with the radio the whole way to the house before realizing I'm jamming out to "Jingle Bell Rock".

Good lord. What has come over me?

As I approach the driveway and circle around, I have one guess as to what's happened.

Amber Crawford has made me like Christmas.

Not love it... but at least I no longer despise it. It's as if these small moments are rebuilding my appreciation for the little things rather than me focusing on the bigger obstacles.

For instance, I should be knee-deep in fiscal numbers, and I haven't opened them once since meeting with Amber a few days ago.

When I walk through the door, the battling smells overload me. Sweet, savory, and if I'm not mistaken, I also smell roasting marshmallows. Gizmo comes flying down the spiral staircase, wearing his own pair of boots with bells on them. They jingle with every step he takes, and it takes me back to Amber flouncing around the decor store. Speak of the elf and she appears.

Amber comes around the corner, her boots clunking on the tile. "Gizmo, where did you—"

She stops short at the sight of me, her mouth dropping, then closing quickly. I can't tear my eyes away from her lips, from the tip of her tongue peeking out to graze the curve of her upper lip. Fleetingly, I wonder what that little niche would feel like under my own tongue's caress. Probably plump and soft.

"Amber."

"Yes?"

"Why in the fuck are you not on your scooter?"

She plants her hands on her hips, swaying a little as she stares up at me defiantly. "I'm not completely down and out, Sebastian. There's plenty to hang on to as I make my way around the house. And what if the scooter scratches your floors?"

"Oh, screw the floors," I growl. "If you fall and get hurt again, I—"

I stop, our eyes locked in a stare, and I'm determined not to finish my sentence or blink before her.

"I'm fine." She clears her throat, breaking our gaze, and inwardly I cheer at my victory. Staring contests are a big deal in the Sterling family. "Now, get in here and taste all the food my mom cooked today, or she's gonna clean both of our plows."

"Clean our what?" I ask. She jerks her head toward me as I'm trying to wrap my mind around her statement. "Clean our plows?"

"Yeah, like... plows on a farm?"

"So..."

"Well, we'll be in trouble. It's an expression."

"What an odd expression," I muse, offering Amber my arm instinctively, and when she links hers through my elbow, holding my bicep with her soft hand, the contact warms my skin immediately. "What have you been doing while your mom cooked all day?"

"I've made lots of phone calls, booked a florist, emailed about someone coming to set up the lights." Amber rambles off as we make our way to the kitchen. "I sampled a few things in between, of course. Quality control. Can't let you try things below standard."

She throws a wink at me before pushing through the saloon-style doors, the absence of her touch leaving my arm cold. As I follow her through, all thoughts of my cold skin are erased and replaced by the magnificent arrangement spread out across the kitchen counters.

There's so much food, I fear Joy didn't leave anything at the grocery store. Platters of cookies and cupcakes in different flavors, sandwiches and dips, and a few things that must be different casseroles. Definitely not what we would normally serve, but the homey aroma, the visual appeal, it's absolutely perfect. And at the center, covered by the glass cake dome I don't think has ever been used in this house, is a pineapple upside-down cake. It's perfect.

I move closer, trailing my fingers over the lid, and notice she used crushed pineapple instead of slices. My words catch in my throat, no sound coming out when I attempt to compliment the masterpiece. The bright red cherries beckon me, the perfect crust of the Bundt cake tempting me more than anything I can remember being a temptation.

"Oh my god, this is so good." Amber moans, and it's as if my head moves in slow motion. She licks icing from the side of a strawberry cupcake, her tongue sweeping it off as if it's second nature, lapping the sugary goodness into her mouth. She licks her lips clean, eyes closed as if she's savoring the flavor, and damn, is it hot in here? I tug at my tie, my collar seeming as if it's two sizes too small.

"Oh, would you like a piece, dear?" Joy bustles over, taking the lid off the cake I was admiring before being distracted by Amber.

What the hell? I've been blind to women for a year, and the

one that I need to succeed with my plan is the first to elicit a physical reaction from me. How lucky is that?

"Sebastian?" Joy taps my forearm, and I snap out of it.

"I'd love a piece, if you don't mind. This is my favorite cake in the world."

Joy flashes me a knowing smile before slicing it up and serving me a piece in no time. I move to the other side of the counter and take a seat on a stool, ready to dive in. I fork up a heaping bite, the brown-sugar crusted fruit glinting at me.

"Phoebe told me this cake was your favorite," Joy calls, her head stuck in the fridge. She emerges with a gallon of milk and a glass, pouring it a little over half-full and setting it beside my plate. The cold milk fogs up the glass, and I'm suddenly transported back in time. I'm six years old, and my mom has made this cake, with crushed pineapples, and poured me a glass of milk after keeping the cup in the fridge all day.

Emotions fill me to the brim, my chest tightening as my shaking hand brings the first bite to my lips. The moment it hits my tongue, I know it's absolutely perfect, and a sip of the milk to wash it down completes the beautiful combination.

Amber slips onto the stool beside me, and we eat our desserts in companionable silence, but as I scrape the crumbs with my fork, she reaches over and squeezes my arm quickly before we move on to the rest of the food.

EIGHT

Amber

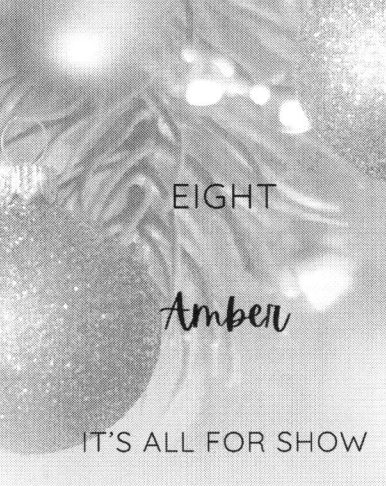

IT'S ALL FOR SHOW

Once we've eaten our fill and decided on a final menu, Sebastian and I help my mom clean up the kitchen. As he finishes loading the dishwasher, I offer to walk Mom to the door.

Well... hobble Mom to the door.

"Are you sure you'll be okay being alone again? I know Sebastian goes back to the city." Mom slips her gloves on, eyes narrowed on me for signs of uncertainty. Does she expect him to take care of me every day?

"I swear, I'll be fine. Gizmo and I will be making phone calls and eating all the leftovers from your day in the kitchen."

"You better not feed my baby too much," she warns me as she buttons up her coat. "We can't have him getting a tummy ache."

"Yes, Mother." I sigh theatrically, grinning at her when she shoots me a look. "I would never make your favorite child ill."

She wraps her arms around me, and I sink into her embrace, inhaling her familiar scent. "You know you're my favorite child, you goober."

"I'm your only child, so not sure that actually counts." Her hair muffles my words, but she still laughs softly.

"Get some sleep, drink lots of water, and for goodness' sake, use the damn scooter." She points at where it's resting against the wall. "I don't think that man cares about his floors at all."

"What is that supposed to mean?"

She gives me a pointed look, then motions in a circle with her hands. "All of this that he's doing. Taking care of you."

"Yeah, because I'm working for him," I remind her, my defenses rising as her words sink in. I've been ignoring this feeling in the pit of my stomach, but my fantasy this morning and the way Sebastian looked at me while I ate my cupcake have me second-guessing everything about this arrangement.

"Phoebe told me he's going to ask you to go to a ribbon cutting with him before your checkup." She lowers her voice to a whisper. "What's that mean?"

"I'm his fake girlfriend, Mom. You know that." I push away the image I conjured up again of the object of our conversation between my legs. "It's all for show."

"If you say so." She shrugs, backing off. "I'll text you when I get home. I love you, sweetheart."

"Good night, Mom."

The door shuts behind her, and I lean on my scooter, her words still rolling around in my mind. I'm not sure what to think or how I feel about most of it, but I do know Sebastian is an attractive man, and I'm not terrible myself.

When two people spend as much time together as we have been, things are bound to happen. That's all it is. The familiarity can be confused for something more, but I am positive it's one-sided. There's no way Sebastian Sterling is dealing with the same thoughts. He's just a chivalrous gentleman, despite his distaste for the holidays. No one's perfect, I suppose.

Speaking of the holidays, it's time for him to decorate

his tree. Propping my knee back up on the scooter, I wheel through the living room and back into the kitchen to find Bash still at the counter, his face bright red. He clears his throat multiple times before I come to a stop at his side, and he takes a long drink of the milk my mom left him.

"You okay?"

His eyes are watering, and he coughs again, tucking his face into his elbow. "So, funny story." He coughs again, which isn't funny. "I'm allergic to pineapples."

Glancing at him, the half-eaten cake, and back at him, my eyes widen in horror. "Sebastian Sterling, you ate half the damn cake, and you're allergic to pineapples?"

"It's the only way I can eat them. Or on pizza. When you cook them, the allergens aren't as strong."

"Oh god. We won't even discuss the travesty that is pineapple on pizza right now. What do we do?"

I carefully bring my injured foot down to the floor, the boot knocking on the tile, and I try not to wince.

"I need Benadryl. About seventy-five milligrams. And I'll be fine," he manages through several more coughs and a throat clearing. "It's in your bathroom above the sink."

Thankfully, my bedroom and bathroom are relatively close, but I can't carry the medicine if I'm riding a scooter.

"Can you walk?"

"Of course I can walk, Amber," he sputters. "Let's go."

I latch onto his arm as he leans on me, and we hobble our way to my bathroom. By the time I lean onto the sink, we're both out of breath, and I don't know if this is exhaustion or his inability to breathe altogether.

"If someone were to see us, they'd laugh their ass off." I pour three pills into my palm. "Open your mouth." He obeys and I cram them inside, then grab the cup I used to rinse my mouth this morning and fill it with water. He downs it in no time, then drops it into the sink.

"You won't be driving home tonight, sir."

"I'll sleep upstairs. I definitely can't drive."

"Oh no. What if you have a rebound reaction or something? You're sleeping with me."

"I didn't know you wanted to be that close to me." He smirks.

"I know the meds didn't hit that quick." I take his arm, and we manage our way back to my bed, where he promptly plops down. He kicks off his shoes and loosens his tie, and as it slips from his neck, I envy the material grazing his skin.

It's going to be a long fucking night.

"I guess we're not decorating a tree tonight." I wrangle myself onto the bed, wrapping up underneath the soft downy comforter. "Maybe we can do it when you get home tomorrow."

"Oh, oh." He flops back on the pillows, his head only missing the wall by mere inches. "I have to cut a ribbon tomorrow at a new shopping center. Would you be able to join me? As my girlfriend," he specifies, glancing at me as if I've forgotten the arrangement.

"Yes, that'll be fine. I don't know if I have anything appropriate to wear for something like that."

"No need. You have an outfit being delivered. Something Phoebe picked out, apparently."

"So, why did Phoebe fail to mention to us that you're allergic to pineapples when we asked her your favorite desserts?"

"She doesn't know. She hasn't worked for me very long, and it's been years since anyone has been here to make one," he mumbles, turning on his side to face me. His eyes are half-closed, and he's so cute lying beside me, completely unguarded and every trace of his stern composure washed away.

"Well, next time tell someone before you just dig in."

"I will if you're careful with that ankle. Use the damn scooter more."

"Fine, deal," I agree in a flash. "But it seems like we're all about making these deals." I laugh. "First the party, then the fake girlfriend thing, now this."

"I guess that's part of it."

"Part of what?"

"The sugar papa thing," he quotes me before his lips curl into a smile. "Get some sleep. We've got a big day of faking it tomorrow."

He drifts off to sleep in no time, and I don't think he moves all night.

I know that because I wake up every ten seconds to check on him.

When the sun peeks through the curtains, I ease out of bed, pleased that my foot doesn't hurt quite as bad when I step down. The doctor said I need to take it easy for a week, but I'm honestly thinking about taking off at full speed.

Surely this is an overreaction, you know?

Sebastian's still snoozing away, Gizmo curled up on his chest like the traitor he is. I grab my phone and make my way to the kitchen, where I snoop through the fridge for something that resembles breakfast.

I'm honestly not in the mood for any of Mom's party samples, but that's about all that's here. Probably because no one actually lives here anymore. From the moment I stepped into the house, that much was obvious—the emptiness, the lack of personal touch. I've ordered décor and decorations, but the homey touch is not something you can buy in a frame to hang on the mantle. It comes from the people that live in a house, that make it their own.

After settling on a glass of apple juice, I shut the fridge and collect a cup from the cabinet. Once I've poured my drink, I settle at the counter, swiping through my phone notifications and social media tags. Ava sent me some photos from her trip. She's out of town for some case. That's all I know. Everything is very hush-hush right now, but I'm hoping she'll eventually tell me what's up.

I'll know when the case goes to court, at least. I'm sure it'll be all over the internet.

Ava won't mind the attention, but she's a bit of a perfectionist. I hope they're not hard on my best friend.

The opening click of a door interrupts my scrolling, and I glance toward the kitchen entrance. The house is so big that it's difficult to discern where some noises come from, but that was the unmistakable sound of a key in the front door.

The doors open and I find myself face to face with Charlotte. Sebastian's ex-fiancée, my ex-boss Charlotte. Although I was just one in a crowd of the party planning committee, I am in her old kitchen in my pajamas. She's dressed to the nines, all smooth and sleek while I have bedhead and sloppy clothes on.

Her gaze roves over me, lips curled into a twisted snarl. "What do we have here?"

She clicks her way over to me in stilettos with heels longer than some of the dicks I've been introduced to before she takes a seat onto the stool next to me, putting her foot up on the legs of mine.

"Are you Sebastian's newest fling, then?"

I try not to flinch at her words, at the insinuation that I'm just another notch on his bedpost. I'm not even a real notch, but that's neither here nor there.

"What are you doing here?" We both jump at the abrupt growl from behind us, where Sebastian looms in the doorway from the bedroom. His hair drips onto his shoulders, and he's in nothing but a towel, hung low around his waist.

And I mean *low*. One wrong blow of the wind, and that towel is letting loose like it's had one too many shots, and while the situation is tense, I can't help but drink in his beautiful form. Tone and tight and tan and just... God, I bet he could give Charlotte's stilettos a run for their damn money.

"Bash, darling," Charlotte squeals, hopping off the stool with so much grace that it makes me feel inferior. "I was just getting acquainted with your little friend here. I didn't catch her name, although you probably haven't, either."

Her dry laugh, her disdain of me mixed with the reminders of how she treated her employees, spurs the vitriol inside me even further.

"Oh, he knows my name. He spent last night screaming it," I quip before downing my apple juice and clinking the glass against the counter.

Both turn to me with hilarious expressions—Charlotte's as if she swallowed a lemon, and Sebastian's as if it's already Christmas morning.

Well, if he loved Christmas like a normal person.

Our gazes meet over Charlotte's head, and his eyes widen theatrically. I flash him a smirk, and he makes his way across the room in two strides before cupping my face in his hands. "Good morning, Angel."

"Morning yourself," I murmur, brushing his nose with mine. His wicked grin sends my stomach into spirals, and all I can think about is how much of his skin is showing. Everything about this is an illusion to spurn Charlotte, but the way his eyes burn into mine, that's not a show or trick. Every inch of my skin is alive, buzzing with anticipation.

"I'd ask how you slept, but I know the answer to that."

His smirk widens at my comment before he presses his lips to my cheek. He cups the nape of my neck, and I keep myself from jumping at the contact just in time. It's been a while since this sleigh had its last ride, and all of Sebastian's attention is a tad overwhelming.

Good overwhelming, but still.

I'd almost forgotten Charlotte by the time she clears her throat.

I sigh. "Oh, you're still here."

"What do you want, Charlotte?" Sebastian turns his body slightly, leaning against the counter. Our arms brush, and then he moves his behind me, his hand finding my hip.

"I thought you might need my help with the party. I canceled my cruise." Her eyes follow his every movement, narrowing the more he touches me.

"Why would I need your help? And why the fuck do you have a key? I changed the locks." Sebastian's tone grows darker and quieter. Somehow that's more threatening than if he'd yelled.

"Because I always plan this event. And I happened across the key."

"You mean you stole it from your dad." He squeezes my hip. "Amber and I are planning the party together." His emphasis on the word together doesn't go unmissed.

"You never helped me with the party, Bash," she whines.

"You didn't want me to. You know I loved Christmas, but you just... took control."

His words surprise me, but I control my features. Sebastian loved Christmas? Wonder what changed his mind. Maybe Charlotte's controlling habits.

"Whatever. It doesn't matter." Sebastian pulls me to his side, and I grip the stool for balance until I'm resting against him. "Get out of my house and leave the key. You can tell Herschel I won't be giving him another copy, thanks to you."

Herschel? Herschel is Charlotte's dad? My heart sinks a bit at the revelation. If he's trying this hard to protect Herschel, maybe he does still have feelings for the snooty woman before us.

She raises her nose in the air, prancing off without another word. The door slams and I maneuver out of Sebastian's hold, something inside me kind of sad.

No matter what, this is all fake. A show.

It tricked Charlotte. I need to keep my distance, or I'll end up tricked, as well.

NINE

Sebastian

STOP BEING A CREEP

After Charlotte's abrupt visit this morning, Amber became much quieter than normal. She played along with the ruse and being that close to her was exhilarating. Now we're in the backseat of the car, Mike at the wheel, and I'm hoping I didn't overstep. Then again, maybe her foot is bothering her.

She only has to keep weight off of it for a few more days, but I know it has to be annoying, not to mention frustrating due to her love for Christmas. She had a million things listed to try to fit in, and this accident made that a tad more difficult.

"After the ribbon cutting, we can do some shopping, if you want. This mall is going to be mind-blowing." I put a piece of candy into my mouth, the crackling of the wrapper seeming to fill the whole car.

Amber glances over at me, nodding with a small smile. "Whatever you wanna do."

"Thanks again for coming with me." I thank her for what feels like the tenth time.

"All part of the plan." She smiles before pulling out her phone, immersing herself in some scrolling.

By the time we reach the mall an hour later, I'm about ready to go back to sleep. Sure, Charlotte believes I didn't get any sleep, but honestly, I slept amazingly and could've probably used some more. I love pineapple upside-down cake, and it's probably dumb to risk eating it, but the Benadryl worked, eh? No worries. And I slept well. A win-win.

"Mr. Sterling, we've arrived," Mike announces once we pull into the new mall parking lot.

The building is beautiful, sleek, and sophisticated, designed in a more modern style than the older ones. Everything is technically open to customers, but for publicity's sake, we do a ribbon cutting. I kind of think they're old fashioned, and the time and money could be spent better elsewhere, but it is what it is. I suppose keeping with tradition is important at times.

"Oh, it's beautiful." Amber perks up, her eyes no longer focused on her phone for the first time in ages. She slept by my side all night, and though I was out for the count, her warmth might have comforted me some, along with the medication.

Once we park, I rush out of the car and open the trunk for her scooter.

"Here are the keys, Mr. Sterling. I'll be in the food court when you're ready," Mike says.

"See you in a bit," I reply over my shoulder, focusing on the task of getting Amber's ride ready. Oh god. Suddenly, my mind fills with the image of Amber riding something a bit taller and grumpier than her scooter...me.

By the time I've wrestled the contraption out onto the ground, she's wobbled over and quickly props herself up on it, pulling her purse up on her shoulder. I push away my carnal thoughts.

"Allow me?" I offer, holding my hand out for her purse. She

narrows her eyes at me before sighing and handing it over, and I promptly throw it into the trunk.

"Sebastian," she growls, a low rumble that catches me off guard. Her pursed lips, the low hum still lingering in her throat, are a shot of exhilaration after her silence. "I need that!"

"I told you, your money's no good here."

"What about my phone?"

Oh, even better. "You're on your phone too much, anyway. Live in the moment."

"Oh, please." She scoffs. "Hello, kettle, I'm pot. You might as well sew yours to your palm."

I toss my phone into the trunk, as well, slamming the lid before I can think twice. "How's that? We're even. You can have your purse when we get home."

"Really? You think so?" Her tone catches me off guard, and I squint at her.

"Yes, I know so."

"Because you're the boss? You've got this under control?"

What is she up to? "Yes, as a matter of fact, I am. I do!" I puff out my chest.

"So tell me, Mr. Boss Man. Are you as good at picking locks as you are commanding everyone around?"

"What?"

"Are you an idiot?" Her harsh words light a match inside me, my amusement at her bordering on something else... not annoyance or anger. Frustration.

"What's that supposed to mean?"

"You just threw the keys into the trunk too." Amber's lips tighten as if she's fighting a smile, and shit, I can't hold mine back, either. Before I know it, the laughter bursts from my lips, and she follows suit, till we're both cackling in the parking lot like a bunch of idiots.

"Anyone... have a... spare key?" she gasps between giggles.

"Yeah, if I could call someone." I clutch my chest, the laughter painful and freeing at the same time.

"Do you have anyone's numbers memorized?" She wipes her eyes, collecting herself, and I follow suit, unable to keep my eyes from her glowing face. She's lit up and happy now, her eyes dancing and her cheeks rosy. Just the way I like her.

Shit. I'm not supposed to like her.

"Um, no. I don't. You?"

She takes off on her scooter, heading into the mall, and I take a few larger steps to keep up with her. At least the snow has melted, and while it's cold, there's not any ice to worry about in the parking lot.

"I would call Ava, but she's out of town. You didn't throw your wallet into the trunk, did you?"

She glances at me, and I stick my tongue out at her. I'm not sure where that came from, but it was instinctual. She bursts out laughing again, and by the time we reach the doors, we're both out of breath between laughing and the walk.

"No, it's right here." I pat my ass, hoping to God it didn't fall out in the back seat or some shit. "Why?"

"Because I need some hot chocolate after this." She shakes her finger at me before we step through the automatic doors. "Now, how long do we have before the ribbon cutting?"

We both move to check our phones, then it's like we remember simultaneously.

"It does seem like I'm missing part of my arm." I flex my fingers, the absence of my device noticeable. "I never realized how... attached I am, I suppose."

"I think that's everyone these days. Guess we're skipping the hot chocolate. We can't be late. Dammit."

As we step onto the carpet, the wheels of Amber's scooter catch on the fabric.

"What the hell." I tug at the handles, trying to pull it loose.

"What kind of dipshit puts carpet in a mall these days?" Amber growls, and we both stop struggling with the scooter and look at each other. "I mean..."

Realization dawns that she's talking about me. I built this mall.

"I don't..." I don't wanna say it because it sounds shitty, but it's true, and Amber takes the words right out of my mouth.

"You don't oversee those details." Amber shrugs. "Let's lose the scooter for now. I'll just lean on you. How far do we have to go?"

Glancing left and right, then left again, I peer through the bustling crowds and spot the elevator sign. "The main office is near the elevator. So that way."

We prop her scooter up on the wall, and I move to the side of her injured foot, letting her lean on me as we push through the crowds.

"Is this not normally how you come in for these things?"

"How'd you guess? Normally, I arrive by helicopter or am already in the building before the mall opens." I tighten my arm around her waist as a surge of teenagers rushes by.

If she fell and hurt something else, I'd kick my own ass. Her ankle, sure, that was different, but this would be on me. On my lack of paying attention to details.

My hand grazes the soft skin where the hem of her blouse meets the waist of her form-fitting black dress pants, and I ignore the blood rushing to my head. How can one small scrap of skin cause such a reaction?

Maybe because you haven't had sex in a year, idiot. Stop being a creep.

As we turn the corner, I realize she's waiting on me to answer. "I'm sorry, what'd you ask?"

"Why is it different this time?"

"Oh, um. Because I wanted you to come." I clear my throat,

relieved that the podium is in sight. "Look, here we are." We press through the remaining people, and after making sure Amber is safely on the stand, I step up myself.

There's a small crowd gathered, and of course, Herschel is front and center, like I knew he would be. Damn the old man. I'm going to have to have a meeting with our planning committee. After all I've done to maintain the peace, to uphold the traditions, I'm sure he won't be pleased. And he had to know his daughter took his key. Surely he wouldn't leave it just lying around. It's like a knife in my back. But I won't pull the blade out yet. I force a smile when his eyes meet mine, and the mall manager approaches us with an outstretched red ribbon.

"Hello, everyone, and welcome to the grand opening of the newest Sterling Mall."

The crowd applauds lazily, and after a scan, I spot a few more investors. Their eyes aren't on me, though; they're on Amber.

She's perched against me, and when I glance over at her, her beauty nearly knocks me over. As if I'm seeing her through their eyes, fresh eyes, instead of as my coworker and fake girlfriend. She's always been pretty, but something about being in the spotlight illuminates her features. Or maybe it's the fact that she's here, supporting me and not putting down everything I like.

She turns her head, our eyes meeting, and the noise of the crowd fades as I study her face. How had I missed it before? I am an idiot.

"You gonna cut the ribbon, Bash?" She nudges me with her elbow, and I turn back to the crowd, taking the giant scissors she passes to me. Everything for the rest of the event is a blur, except Amber's shining face.

By the time it's over and I've shaken hands with everyone, I'm refocused, and my mind is clear again. The crowd slowly disperses, and I take Amber's hand in mine as we make our way back through the mall. She doesn't pull away, letting me wrap her fingers in mine. My heartbeat drums in my palm, and I swear she can probably feel it too.

"So, how are we getting back into the car, sugar papa?" she jokes as I lead her to the food court, my eyes peeled for the coffee shop.

"Well, first things first, we're going to have that hot chocolate you were wanting." I squeeze her hand gently as we come to a stop, the aroma of cinnamon and freshly ground beans filling the air. "Then, if you want to do some shopping before your checkup, we can, and I'll call Mike from the mall office."

"Your mall has carpet. Are you sure you don't have pay phones?" She elbows me, and while she's joking, it does give me a few ideas.

"Don't you worry, I've got some plans for all our malls. Now, you sit here." I gently lead her to a table for two and ease her into the seat. "I'll grab your drink, and we'll get busy with our day."

"Oh, you didn't—"

"A large hot cocoa with whipped cream and chocolate chips," I rattle off, remembering her declaration from earlier. Her smile tugs at my heart strings, and I turn on my heel before she can see my cheeks redden.

What kind of sugar daddy blushes, after all?

TEN

Amber

I'M DONE WITH SEXY TALK

"I'm gonna order one more X-ray, just as a precaution, but I think you should be good to go." Dr. Ridgestone clasps his hands together, glancing between Sebastian and me. "I do have to ask..."

He pauses, and nothing could prepare me for what comes out of his mouth next. I should have known because it's normal in times like these, but with the ribbon cutting and the car debacle, and everything in between, it's just... It's been a damn day.

He sighs. "Is there any chance you could be pregnant, Ms. Crawford?"

His glance between us now makes perfect sense, and while I know they have to ask, the thought of admitting it in front of Bash is semi-embarrassing. He's going to think no one wants me.

Screw that. I'm a strong, independent woman, fully capable of delivering my own orgasms. If I wanted to be with someone, I would be.

"No chance at all."

"Are you on birth control?" The doc clears his throat, and I'm like damn, he's really going all out here. He could've pulled up my chart. I'm sure it's on there.

My reply is more diplomatic out loud, of course. No need to cause a scene. "Yes, but I'm also currently abstinent."

"Alright, then. You just need to take it a little easy the next week or so, but you can drop the scooter and the boot now. We'll send you over for an X-ray, and I'll call you if I see anything going on."

"Thanks, doc." Sebastian shakes his hand, and we still haven't looked at each other. Maybe he doesn't feel as awkward as I do discussing these things in front of each other. I mean, we've seen each other at our worst possible moments in the last week, so I guess it's not that big of a deal.

Maybe it's a bigger deal because of the way my stomach squirms and my skin heats when I remember my dream. Oh god. The dream. And I used that dream in the most delicious way.

Clenching my thighs together to soothe the ache growing between them, I gather my belongings from the chair and move to my feet. The doc holds the door open for us, and I lead the way out after Sebastian motions to me. "Ladies first."

As he follows behind me, his nearness makes the hairs on my arms stand on edge. It's like my body knows where he is every second, and all my thoughts are a jumble so that by the time we reach the X-ray room and I hand him my belongings, I'm out of breath from more than just the walk.

He takes my belongings, staring down at them for a moment, then back at me with a furrowed eyebrow.

"You can't go in there. Can I trust you not to lock that shit into the trunk this time?"

"Why the hell can't I go in there?" Suddenly, he's towering over me, as if his aggravation made him two feet taller, his broad shoulders tightening against the fabric of his suit. God, to watch him unbutton that dress shirt would just put the cherry on top of this moment.

"Chill out, dude. The rays could turn you into an X-Men character or some shit."

"Well, what about you?"

"They'll put this protective apron thing over me."

"Amber, you're sorely mistaken if you think I'm letting you out of my sight." His eyes bore into mine, his lips slightly parted as though he's waiting to counter my argument.

"I mean, we can ask. I'll be fine, though."

At that moment, the door opens behind us, revealing the tech with a clipboard as big as my face. Damn, I need one of those for this party planning shit. My mouth opens to ask where I can get one that size, when my mind travels to sizes of different *things* and the innuendo that could be insinuated if I word that the wrong way.

After the birth control stuff, I'm done with sexy talk. Not that birth control is actually sexy, but you catch my drift.

"Ms. Crawford, we're ready to take your scans now." She pushes her glasses up on her nose, her eyes darting between Sebastian and me. "Your friend can wait out here."

"Excuse me." Sebastian turns on the charm, flashing a thousand-watt smile at the tech that makes me wish I had some damn sunglasses. I've never seen him so friendly. It's a bit disconcerting.

"I'd like to come in during the X-ray, please. I'll wear one of your vests, of course, and I can sign a waiver. Whatever is needed. I just..." He sighs, closing his eyes for a moment and then opening them to reveal watery pupils. What a fucking liar! "I can't bear to let her do any of this alone. I know it's a lot to ask, but I love this hospital. That's why I sponsor so many things here."

"Oh, okay. Just this once, Mr. Sterling. But only because you asked so nicely." Shit, she's probably not accustomed to that at all. She steps back, waving us in and shutting the door closed behind us. As she passes both of us a radiation apron, she whispers, "And mainly because of the employee quiet room."

"Oh, you love the solar lights, the natural furniture, all that good stuff?" Sebastian covers himself with the apron as I roll my eyes at him, the devious glint in his eyes actually endearing. He's all puffed up and proud, like the cat that ate the canary.

"I think it turned out beautifully." I reassure Sebastian about his homemade ornament while making my own, my fingers itching carefully to place another tiny bead on the hot glue.

Holding it in place, I chance a look over at my partner in holiday crime. Sebastian is holding his ornament up by its ribbon, his lip curled up in distaste.

When I told him my price for today's ceremony was making ornaments, he took it in stride. Maybe because he still felt bad about locking the keys in the trunk or stealing my phone, but whatever the reason, he was almost... well, not excited, but at least happy as we gathered supplies and Googled instructions on our phones.

It was almost odd to have my phone in my hand again, and I even muted some of the notifications before we started. If there's an emergency, my mom could always contact me for anyone, and I wouldn't say it out loud, but I am kind of enjoying the peace and quiet, the absence of constant dings and whistles. I'd never admit it, but him throwing my shit into the trunk kind of made the day better. Otherwise, I would've been taking pictures of everything and missed out on things I actually saw.

"Oh, you look so grumpy," I say, careful not to shake my work of art. I don't want the beads flying off. I'm sure it's not dry yet.

"I do not," Sebastian bristles, the ribbon slipping a little out of his grasp, and he tightens his hold before it can hit the table. I could imagine the glitter flying everywhere.

This man absolutely despises glitter and the holidays, and everything spirited... or I thought he did. After Charlotte's little slip this morning, I know better, and it's time to start teasing him, get him to show his true colors. Something upsets him about the holidays, but dude, it's in the past, and we're gonna move on and throw an amazing party without Her Royal Highness.

Part of me still thinks Sebastian has a lingering flame for her, and if that's the case, I don't want to fuck it up for him. Even if there's an odd pain in my stomach at the thought of him in her arms. I didn't have the best experiences with her, but something about her has to be okay for Sebastian to have almost married her. Right?

I clear my throat, gathering all the ornaments I've made for a quick last look. "Ready to decorate the tree?"

"Yeah, sure thing." We push back from the table at the same time, our chairs screeching across the floor. "I can't wait to see the tree lit up tonight. It'll really brighten up the place." Sebastian handles his balls carefully as we make our way into the living room, and I have another sexy thought... How does he handle his more sensitive pair?

There's something absolutely wrong with me. It'll all shift back to normal when I move back home tomorrow. Ava comes home tonight, and my foot is perfectly fine, just a twinge every now and then.

There's no further reason for me to stay here at Sebastian's house.

And to be frank, the whole thing is nuts, anyway. We're practically strangers.

Except now he knows how I drink my coffee or hot chocolate, and I know his morning routine. Protein drink, workout, shower, breakfast. You can set your clock by Sebastian Sterling's pre-work rituals. And I'm sure he's ready to go back home, as well.

"How about some music while we work?" Sebastian suggests, having already set his decorations down on the side table gently, he's now scrolling through his phone.

The speakers in the corners blare to life, Bing Crosby's husky bass filling the room with "I'm Dreaming of a White Christmas".

"Oh, this was always my favorite song."

"It is a beautiful one," I agree, carefully hanging some of my ornaments from the upper limbs of the tree. There's no way I'll be able to reach the top, but I'll stretch as high as I can.

The rest of the room was decorated while we were gone today, and now wreaths and mistletoe are spread throughout the room. Upon Sebastian's request, I didn't order any cinnamon to be used anywhere in the house. While the main lights are off, the strands are all shining brightly, and the house has a completely different atmosphere than when I first came here.

Then, it was empty, as if a ghost lived here, but now it's warm and comforting. It feels more and more like a home every day. Not my home, obviously. But *a* home, just comfortable and relaxing.

As I hang my last ornament, a hand covers mine, our skin bright against the pine needles. Then Sebastian's hand wraps around mine, pulling me into his arm, but not against his body.

Thank goodness. I'm not sure how my body would react to that. There's a polite amount of distance between our bodies, and Sebastian leads me into a slow dance.

"It's so beautiful here." I interrupt the silence, attempting a normal conversation. "The decorators did a fantastic job."

"They did." Sebastian dips his head in agreement, eyes burning into me. "You planned it all, though. I can't thank you enough for everything, Amber. I know I have been a bit of a scrooge."

Laughter slips from between my lips before I can stop it, and he watches me curiously. "What's so funny?"

"Scrooge's biggest fault wasn't his disdain for the holidays. I mean, yeah, that's a big deal in the story, but the worst part was he was so selfish. He didn't care if people were poor or hungry or healthy. So, no, you're not a scrooge."

We take another turn around the living room, the space between us beckoning me. I want to lean in, to see if my head fits in the perfect crook of his shoulder and neck, and maybe he'll pull his arms tighter around me.

"A grinch, then?"

"Hmm?"

"If I'm not a scrooge, perhaps I'm a grinch."

Pulling back and breaking our rhythm, I pretend to survey him carefully from head to toe for a moment. "Well, you're not green and furry." Gizmo barks his opinion from the couch, his ears narrowed, and I chuckle. "You do have a little sidekick, though. Gizmo would look cute with antlers."

The song ends and we drop our arms immediately, but there's a chill on my skin in the absence of Sebastian's warmth. He moves quickly, hanging his ornaments and decorations on the tree. Watching him is amusing, the way he steps back and admires his handiwork with his hands on his hips. His transformation has been almost grinch-like, although he wasn't out to destroy the holidays, really.

The image is suddenly crystal clear, and it's all I can take to refrain from squealing with delight. Sebastian's head turns slowly, his eyes narrowing as he surveys my face.

"What are you thinking?" His hand is still poised to hang an ornament on the tree.

"What do you mean?" Willing my pulse to calm down, I flash him a winning smile.

"I'd know that look anywhere. It has ended up planning quite a bit of this shindig."

Unable to stop myself, I let out a bark of laughter. "Oh, you have no clue."

"So, what's the big idea this time?"

He finishes with his last ornament, and then we both take a seat on the couch. I curl my legs underneath me, sticking my tongue out at Gizmo as he automatically moves to Sebastian's lap. Traitor.

"We should have a costume theme!"

"At a formal event?" Sebastian scoffs. "I don't see my stuffy group going for that. And it might be uncomfortable to go around all evening dressed up in crazy costumes."

My heart sinks, a little pain cracking through my chest. Maybe Sebastian does see me as nothing more than a means to an end. The past few days, I got the feeling it was different, but now I'm not sure. Then again, of course he cares what everyone thinks. That's the whole point of this.

"Yeah, you're probably right. I was just thinking you dressed up as a grinch Santa with Gizmo dressed as Max? That would be super cute. The kids would love it!"

His head snaps toward me. "Kids? Amber, kids don't attend this party."

The silence that follows seems to deepen and widen, with Sebastian and I still staring into each other's eyes.

"B-but on the guest list, it had the kids listed. I invited everyone's children. One of them has twelve." Why in the hell is my voice so squeaky? Obviously, I'm just emotional.

"You invited all of them," he repeats. "All the kids."

"Everyone's kids."

ELEVEN

Sebastian

SHE CAN STAY FOREVER

Amber's bottom lip quivers, her eyes staring up at me wide and full of tears. Oh my. "What are we going to do? The party's next week. We've already finalized everything."

"Well, it looks like we're going to have a big ass party with everyone, and it'll be great." Something in me wants to comfort her, to reassure her, but I'm not sure how she'd feel about that, and I would never want to make things awkward. She's upset enough as it is.

"What are we going to do with the kids?" It hits me then, the image of a bunch of rambunctious children running around my spotless house with their sticky hands and faces. And something about the way she asks me, as if they're our kids, creates an odd battle inside me. The empty bedroom upstairs that I always imagined as a nursery suddenly beckons me, all my boxes of childhood toys calling to me.

"Well, how many will there be?"

"At least twenty. Maybe thirty. If everyone shows up." Amber pulls out her phone and opens her notes app.

"What do kids like to do?"

"Um. Video games, I assume," she says as she types. "Pizza? What teenager doesn't like pizza, am I right?"

"Kids love those bouncy house things," I muse, recalling different ideas I've seen for entertainment at the malls. Everyone is always throwing some new kid entertaining thing. If the kids are happy, the parents will shop longer.

"A bouncy house? That's not too extravagant?"

"We're having ice sculptures in the yard. Surely the kids can have a bouncy house to keep them busy. It'll keep their parents happy, too, because they'll be entertained."

"Fair point," Amber agrees, locking her phone with a sigh. "It'll all work out. It has to."

She fiddles with her fingers, intertwining them, then flipping them over so that they're free again. Before I can second-guess myself, I take one of them in my own, and our fingers interlock as if it's the most natural thing in the world.

"You're amazing. You've taken a disaster and turned it into something amazing in no time." My words pour out without a second thought, no overanalyzing, no concern for how she'll react. Every moment I spend with Amber, it's as if another hard piece of my exterior melts away. "And at this point, I don't care if anyone's happy about how the party goes, as long as you are."

The hitch of her breath echoes around me. "That means a lot to me, Bash. It really does. Because I don't want to disappoint you."

"Disappoint me? You could never." The words are laced with emotion, weaved into every syllable and pouring straight from my heart, because it's one hundred percent true.

We're mere inches from each other, and it's like a magnet is pulling me closer. The lights dance in Amber's eyes, and she licks her lips before closing them, her face turned toward me.

She's giving me every signal in the book, and I want to kiss her more than anything in the world.

I close the distance between us with my own eyes barely cracked, her breath grazing my lower lip just as an abrupt sound explodes from between us, as if something's being smothered or attacked.

We jump away from each other and Gizmo emerges, fur flying and eyes wide. He jumps off the couch, shaking himself, and glares back at us before taking off toward the bedroom.

My heart pounds in my chest, from exhilaration and excitement about the kiss but also from the noise and commotion.

"Guess we squashed him a little." Amber grins. "Oops."

"Yes, oops," I agree, although internally, I'd like to rewind time and kick Gizmo off the couch a few seconds earlier. Then I'd be devouring Amber's mouth.

But now she's yawning, stretching her hands over her head, and I'm thinking the moment has indeed passed. "Ready for bed?" I offer.

"I think I might be. And I still have to pack." She moves to her feet, grabbing her phone and tucking it into her back pocket. I jump to my feet, as well, the word alarming me.

"Pack?" The one word is all I can manage without sounding gruff, my voice not quite ready for neutral conversation.

"Yeah, well, Ava came home tonight. And I've been enough of an inconvenience here. I know you're more than ready for a night at your apartment with no one else."

She laughs, and now that I'm looking down at her, I wish I could throw her over my shoulder, take her upstairs, and tell her to have whichever bedroom she likes. She can stay forever and keep me company. The house is so much more bearable. The holiday is even fun with her.

"You can stay as long as you want to. I hope I've made that

clear," I say, following as she heads through the kitchen, padding across the floor to the refrigerator as if she belongs here. "We still have more setup and such. It might be easier to stay here, anyway."

"I'll keep that in mind." Amber sips her juice, then refills the cup again, bringing it with her as she heads toward her room.

I'm in the middle of the kitchen, trying my hardest to reach some decisions, when Amber stops right in front of me. The first time I looked down at her flashes before my eyes in that damn cinnamon-overloaded store, with those damn elf shoes on. It's crazy how much has happened since then, and overwhelming to think it's not over yet.

"Good night." Amber stands on her tippy toes, pressing a kiss to my cheek. "Thank you for everything."

As she steps away, the warmth on my cheek soaks in, barely a trace of her touch lingering, but it's still there. I can feel it. She heads to her bedroom, shuts the door behind her, and I stare at the door longer than necessary. I even consider knocking, bringing her into my arms, and taking a second chance at kissing her.

Gizmo has grown on me, but dammit, I wish I had remembered he was sitting between us. I'm not on allergy meds now, so I'll be sleeping upstairs. Not in the room Charlotte and I shared—I haven't decided on a use for it yet—but in one of the other bedrooms.

The room Amber is using was converted for my father when he became ill, and several times, I've considered remodeling it. I'm thankful we left it as is, because it's proven useful, and you never know when an accident will happen. Like spraining your ankle in the snow. I chuckle at the memory now, even though in the moment it scared me half to death.

Amber certainly is one of a kind.

The spiral staircase is decorated as well now, ribbons and fresh garland winding through the rails. Before I take the first step, the creak of Amber's door opening squeals through the otherwise silent house.

"Everything okay?" I call, not wanting to intrude, but also, I have to make sure nothing's wrong.

She appears in the doorway, now adorned in her pajama shorts and tank top, her hair flowing loosely over her shoulders. She's the most beautiful thing I've ever seen, all comfort and kindness, and I'm across the room, standing in front of her, in no time.

"Amber," I breathe, cupping her soft face in my palms, my thumb tracing her cheekbone.

She nods once, her small smile reaching inside me, wrapping my heart in a safe promise I'm not sure I'm ready for. But it's too late to go back now.

Our mouths meet in a soft, sweet kiss. Our lips move together gently. She's so soft and vulnerable in a way I've never seen her before, and I'm afraid one wrong move will break the spell, break her and send her running in the opposite direction.

She ends our kiss, and I hesitate before opening my eyes. When I open them, we'll have to have a conversation, right? She might decide this complicates things too much, or any other combination of the horrible responses flying around in my head.

"That was interesting," she murmurs, leaning her face against my palm while she looks up at me with a pleased expression on her face. Her eyes are tired, though. It has been a big day.

"Interesting?" That could mean a hell of a lot. Interesting could be a beating-around-the-bush way of saying bad. God. Searching her face for a clue, I find none that insinuate this was a bad decision.

"Unexpected," she amends.

So, I roll with my instincts, covering Amber's mouth with my own again. She whimpers in surprise but returns my kiss enthusiastically. Our mouths are less careful now, our hands friendlier.

She skims her fingers across my chest, around my neck, and then interlocks her fingers at the nape before pulling herself flush against my body. Every curve and valley of her warm, supple body molds into mine, and my skin ignites, aflame with desire and intrigue.

"Okay, that was more than interesting." Her breathless tone is music to my ears, her flushed cheeks and swollen mouth evidence of my triumph.

"Bash."

"Don't." I recognize the warning in her tone. "Don't overthink this. I'm the overthinker, remember? And I'm not second-guessing anything."

"Nothing? Not the fact that we're working together, and I'm your fake girlfriend?"

"It changes nothing about you working for me. The party's next week, and you'll no longer be working with me. Problem solved, if that's your concern."

"And the fake girlfriend thing?"

"Well, just be my real girlfriend. Try that on for size."

"And if it's a bad fit?"

My heart clenches, but I get what she means. Sometimes things happen. "If it's the wrong fit, we can part peacefully as friends. But Amber, I have a feeling we're going to be the perfect match."

"What makes you say that?"

I point up, and she follows my finger until we're both staring at a mess of mistletoe hung above the doorway.

This time, she kisses me first, pressing herself against me as our mouths savor every moment, the tree lights sparkling around us. Even if this season is temporary, I want to soak up every moment.

TWELVE

Amber

AMBER CRAWFORD DOESN'T GET NERVOUS

While staying with Sebastian hasn't been terrible by any means, it's a relief to be able to walk up the stairs, through the door, and settle on my own couch. I kick off my shoes, unabashedly prop my feet onto the arm of the couch, and sigh. Not a normal ladylike sigh, either. A full-on raspberry, exhaling all of the thoughts plaguing me today.

Gizmo curls up on my lap, settling in with a huff of his own.

"Oh, Giz. It's good to be home."

His soft yip makes me smile, even if he's been a traitor over the past week and taken up with Sebastian. Not that I can blame him. Obviously, I've become fond of my fake boyfriend myself.

Well, ex-fake boyfriend?

Now, he's... I don't know what he is, but I do know I enjoyed making out with him by tree light for several minutes before we bid each other goodnight. We could have moved faster. The spark was there, but something in me wanted to wait. Sometimes anticipation makes the reward even sweeter.

Although I have no doubts Sebastian will be excellent in bed either way.

When I left his house this morning, the whole place was silent, and his car wasn't in the garage, so I assumed he'd gone to work for the day. My mom left my car here for me when the time came. I'd considered packing all my stuff and heading home to stay, but he wasn't wrong about being there to plan the party. And it won't hurt to be close to Sebastian. Who knows when more mistletoe will be hanging around.

The creaking of a door followed by familiar padding of feet precede Ava emerging from the hallway, her hair piled in a messy bun on top of her head. She raises my legs up and sinks into the cushion beside me, scooting as close to me as she can before setting my legs down gently again.

She puts her head on my shoulder. "I missed you, Bambi."

"I missed you, Ava." I lean my head on hers, my body relaxing as the comfort of being home with my best friend washes over me. "Tell me about your trip. It feels like we haven't talked in years."

"Oh god. Don't even get me started." She shudders. "Tell me about your stay at Château Sterling. Did the grinch's heart grow three sizes while you were there? Did something else grow too?"

I gasp at her mockingly. "Ava! But really, you know, I think his heart did. He helped me decorate the tree, and we made ornaments."

"That's a lot of holiday cheer for someone so opposed to the idea originally."

"Well, his ex showed up the other morning."

Ava pops up, knocking her head against my jaw.

"Ouch." I rub my face, opening my mouth and moving my jaw around. Ava rubs the top of her head, glaring over at me.

"You have a hard fucking face."

"My face? Your head did all the damage, thank you."

"You just dropped a huge info bomb on me. Now, let me grab a snack. You've got to spill the deets." Ava hops up and sprints to the kitchen in warp speed to grab her Cheese Balls before settling onto the couch again.

I shake my head. "You and those damn Cheese Balls."

"You shut the hell up about my Cheese Balls." She narrows her eyes at me as she twists off the lid of the jar. It's half as tall as she is, for god's sake. "Now, out with it. The ex showed up…"

"Fine. But don't you be crunching too loud. It distracts me," I warn her. "So, I woke up before Sebastian the other morning and went to the kitchen to have breakfast and all that good stuff. Next thing I know, someone's coming into the house, and suddenly, Charlotte is standing in the doorway, watching me drink my apple juice."

"Were you in your pajamas?"

"I totally was. I looked awful. It had been a rough night, when Sebastian ate the damn cake he was allergic to, and I was afraid he was going to asphyxiate all night."

"Oh, so you didn't asphyxiate." She wiggles her eyebrows at me.

I grab a cheese ball from her jar and toss it at her. "Stop it, you dirty-minded racoon. No. We haven't done that."

"But you've done something?"

"Would you let me tell the damn story?"

Ava crunches another handful, her fingers now bright orange, and I shudder to think of her touching the furniture. I know she won't. Ava's a huge neat freak, which is why it's so odd that she loves the messiest snacks.

"Get the hell on with it, then."

"So, Sebastian shows up in nothing but his towel, wondering why Charlotte is there, how she had a key, and realizes she must have stolen Herschel's."

"How would she—"

"Because Herschel is her dad!" I exclaim, enjoying Ava's gasp. "And there's more. Apparently, Charlotte never let Bash help plan this party, but... he loved Christmas."

Ava's jaw drops, cheese dust stuck in one corner. Her reactions are priceless, and I've always enjoyed sharing stories with her but haven't had a good one in a while.

"Wait. Is he trying to make Herschel happy because of Charlotte?"

Her mind goes exactly where mine did at first, but I refuse to let the thought dampen my mood.

"I won't lie, the thought crossed my mind, but... last night, we kissed. I mean like, made out under the mistletoe after slow dancing by the Christmas tree. Full of romance." I sigh, the memory of twirling around the room in his arms, of his lips on mine, still fresh in my mind, his fingerprints still burning into my skin.

"So now what?" The snap of the lid fastening onto her jar startles me out of my memory.

"Hmm?"

"I mean, how is it going to work now? The fake boyfriend, party throwing shit."

"We really didn't talk about it last night. And I honestly don't know. My head is all over the place. Like, obviously the party is going as planned, and maybe we just see where things go?"

"You think that's a good idea?"

"From your tone, I assume you don't."

"Damn straight I don't. Without lines, without boundaries, this could take a wrong turn faster than you without your GPS."

"I just... I don't wanna pressure him or anything. Maybe it was just a kiss."

"Maybe. But with Sebastian Sterling, I don't think anything is just simple."

"What makes you say that?"

"He moved you into his house when you sprained your ankle. The man is the king of overboard. He just hasn't let that whole side of him loose yet."

"You might be right."

"Oh, I know I'm right." Ava pulls her phone out of her pocket, and she quickly swipes away a message, rolling her eyes as she does so.

I don't ask who it is; I know better with her. While I like to be asked about things and prodded for information, she likes to let things soak before revealing her feelings and thoughts. She'll come to me if she really has something to talk about. She pulls up the website for our apartment complex and logs in.

"What am I looking at?" I let her handle all that shit and normally just give her cash. For a panicked moment, I think I forgot to give her this month's rent, but that can't be right. I did that when Sebastian paid me for the party.

"I logged in to pay our rent… but it's paid up for six months, Bambi." She zooms in on the next due date, which, true to her word, is next summer.

"Oh my god. You don't think…?"

"Who else would have done it? He's taking this sugar daddy thing even more seriously now, apparently. Must have been some kiss."

The idea of him paying my rent after we kissed leaves a nasty feeling in the pit of my stomach, our moment now almost tarnished by the act.

S: Be ready by five. I have a surprise for you.

I haven't talked to the dude in almost twenty-four hours, and this is the first text I get? I'm not sure how to respond or how to bring up the rent thing, but the biggest concern right now is that I need to know what to wear. Even when I plan our outings, I forget what to wear, and this time I don't want to be caught off guard. I don't think we've had one outing go normally, between my sprained ankle, locking the keys in the car, and Charlotte's impromptu visit.

Me: What should I wear?

S: To start with, very warm layers.

Me: To start with?

S: Who knows where the night will take us, Angel.

Me: Are you flirting with me?

S: Do you want me to flirt with you?

Do I? After the kiss, yes. I would've been more than happy to reciprocate in the flirtatious texting. I guess we'll see how the night goes first.

Me: See you at five.

Ava's gone to work, so I raid her closet for something cute and warm to wear. All of my winter clothes are super cheesy or fall under: comfort but not cute. Two minutes before five, I'm finally ready to go. I pose before Gizmo, showing off the cute leggings and sweater.

"Hopefully, Sebastian isn't as harsh of a critic as you are. Put that lip up."

Gizmo snarls again, followed by a courageous yip.

"That's better. You know I look good." I scratch his ears as a reward for his loyalty before heading to the door.

I stop at the coat rack to load up with my coat, scarf, and gloves. My purse is still on the floor by the door, where I dropped it when I got home yesterday, so I pull it over my shoulder and blow Gizmo a goodbye kiss.

"Be nice to your aunt Ava while I'm gone." He snuggles into the couch, covering his face with his paw. Does that mean he will be? Who knows. He likes to make messes when Ava babysits him.

Just as I'm reaching for the handle, our doorbell echoes throughout the apartment. It's always been loud as fuck, which I'm grateful for. We can hide from unwanted guests if we're in our rooms when it goes off.

Jamming my eye against the peephole, my body hums to life at the sight of Sebastian standing outside, dressed in normal clothes rather than his usual suit and tie, with a bouquet of flowers. He shows no signs of being nervous. He just waits, cool and collected, for me to open the door.

A million years pass with me staring at the doorknob, butterflies throwing a rave in my stomach. Sure, last night was amazing, the picture of everything a girl could dream of, but sometimes a second look reveals cracks and dulled colors. Maybe it's not the masterpiece we thought it was.

Taking a deep breath, I throw the door open before I second-guess myself any longer, and Sebastian's face erupts into a magnificent smile. Even his eyes light up, and the difference between this man and the one who walked into the store at the mall two weeks ago is astounding.

"You look…" He glances over me before making it back up to my face again. *Ha, Gizmo. Told you, you little shit.* "You look beautiful."

"Thank you. So do you. Well. You know what I mean." My cheeks flush, and it hits me that I am a bit nervous. Amber Crawford doesn't get nervous. I'm not sure how I feel about it, but before I can overanalyze, Sebastian hands me the flowers. The arrangement of poinsettias and paperwhites is breathtaking, and it's obvious Sebastian asked for someone to make a holiday arrangement. His thoughtfulness, his regard for my love of the holiday he's leary of, softens something inside me.

"Let me put these in water before we go. Come on in."

His footsteps seem much louder than mine as we make our way to the kitchen, where I search under the sink for the vase Ava used to put flowers in that her ex bought her. She hated flowers, but he still brought them.

"Hey, Giz," Sebastian greets Gizmo, taking a seat on the couch beside him.

Well, shit. Aren't we getting out of here?

Gizmo whines appropriately until Sebastian scratches his ears, then he grumbles happily at the contact. He army crawls onto Sebastian's lap, and to my utter dismay, Sebastian scoops him up. We're never leaving now.

"Would you like a drink before we go?"

"No, thank you. I'm ready when you are."

Gizmo peeks at me from underneath his hair, eyes narrowed and ready for battle. Sebastian caresses him almost absentmindedly. "Where's Ava?"

"Working. Again. She should be home in an hour or so. She'll take care of Giz till I'm back."

"He doesn't mind being left alone?"

"Oh, he hates it. But it'll be okay for a little while. I'll leave Buffy on for him. Oh, speaking of. Has your cat been okay while you stay with me?" I suddenly remember the puffy white furball in the photo he sent me.

"You've never had a cat, have you?"

"Um. No."

"They like being left alone for the most part. I stop by and see her on my lunch and stuff like that. I could bring her to stay at the house, though," he muses. "Wonder how she and Gizmo would get along."

"Gizmo's never met a cat. It would be interesting. Let me turn on the television for him." I head to my room, thankful that Sebastian came to the door. If I'd forgotten to turn it on, Gizmo would have definitely left a mess, and Ava would have been pissed to come home to it.

After switching on the TV, I scroll through the episodes until I find *Wild at Heart*. Sure enough, the little patter of Gizmo running follows shortly, and he hops onto my bed, focused on the screen intently and Sebastian all but forgotten. I turn and find him standing at my door, his own gaze on the screen. "That's such a sad episode."

"It is," I agree. "It's also our favorite."

"You like being sad?"

"No, it's just... I don't know how to explain it."

"Hmm." Sebastian's eyes darken, his features no longer lit up like earlier, and I don't want to put a damper on our evening.

"Alright, let's get going." I lean over and plop a kiss on Gizmo's head.

It's as if I can sense Sebastian's closeness before he actually touches me, the heat from his body emanating around me, and by the time his hand wraps around mine, acceptance has settled in my chest. This is happening, and I want it to.

He pulls me to him, his arm slipping around my waist and our torsos pressed together so tightly you couldn't slip a ribbon between us. I lift my head, our eyes meeting. I expect Sebastian to kiss me, but instead, he buries his head in my neck, both arms wrapped tightly around me. Hesitantly, I wrap my own arms around his neck, interlocking my hands at the base of his neck.

We stand like that for a while, frozen in time, our hearts beating as one. When Sebastian releases his grip, emerging from my shoulder, his eyes have lightened again, and he gives me a sheepish smile.

"Sorry."

"Don't be sorry, please," I insist. "We all need a hug sometimes. It's human nature to want to be close to someone."

"Not even just human nature." He nods toward the TV. "Ready for your surprise now?" He changes the subject, and I don't press the issue. Maybe he's like Ava. He'll tell me if he wants to talk about what just happened.

"Ready." We head out and I lock up behind us, more curious than ever to see what Sebastian Sterling has planned for me. So far, the night has been full of surprises.

THIRTEEN

Amber

YOU WANT ME TO RIDE WITHOUT PANTS?

"Can I look now?"

Sebastian was determined to keep the whole evening a surprise, so much so that he tied my scarf around my eyes as a blindfold. And while I've never been into anything super kinky, I have to admit it's exhilarating, the lack of vision, his hand firmly around mine as we walk wherever we're going.

I do know we're still outside, because the cold evening air is freezing my now bare neck. A shiver runs through me, from excitement or cold, maybe both, but Sebastian must notice.

"Not yet. And you're cold." A warmth wraps around the nape of my neck, the skin-to-skin contact sending a rush of heat throughout my body, and the realization that he's now guiding me by the neck tears me all to pieces. With every step I take, my leggings rub my lady bits, and by the time he stops, I fear I'll explode right now.

His hands move to the scarf, working at the knot, and I can't let the night go further without addressing the Rudolph of this sleigh.

"Wait." I reach behind me and cover his hands with my own. "Before we do this, I need to ask you about something."

"Okay." His voice deepens, the concern evident, and I don't want to worry him, but I have to bring it up. "Ask me."

"Did you pay my rent for six months?" I blurt out the question before I can second-guess.

He doesn't reply for a moment, then finally, "I did."

The heaviness in my heart catches me off guard, as if the ship has dropped anchor. "Because we kissed?"

He turns me so quickly, I lose my balance, and though my eyes are still covered, I can imagine him in front of me, his minty breath all around me as he talks.

"What? No. I did that when you hurt your ankle. I just wanted to help out, and I didn't want you using the money I already paid you for the party. We didn't know the extent of your injury, or if you would need anything long term."

The anchor lifts then, relief flooding me, and my chest is no longer tight. "Oh, thank God."

"While I very much enjoyed our kiss, and I look forward to doing it again sometime, hopefully soon, I wouldn't have done that for a kiss. I don't want to buy your affections, Amber. If you fall for me, I want it to be genuinely for me, not for my money."

His hand finds my neck again, pulling me toward him, and when his lips cover mine, kissing me thoroughly, a sigh of contentment escapes into his mouth.

When we break our kiss, he unties the scarf, the light of the area blinding me. I squint through narrowed eyes, turning to survey where we're at.

My gasp seems to echo over the ice as I take in the beautifully decorated area of the National Gallery of Art Sculpture Garden, the ice skating rink illuminated by the ropes and strands of white lights.

I squeal, sinking against his warmth. "Oh, this is my favorite place to ice skate. Sebastian, this is better than anything I could have imagined."

He takes my hand and leads me to the closest bench before pulling out two pairs of ice skates. "I know you were so disappointed we couldn't go the day you hurt your ankle, and I couldn't let you miss your favorite part of the holidays after you've worked so hard to help me enjoy them."

"You are so sweet." I take the skates, leaning over to peck him on the cheek. "Underneath all that grumpiness, that is."

"Hey now, the grinch can come back," he warns me, smiling playfully as we tie up our laces. "Now, you do have to take it easy. We don't need any more accidents this year."

"Next year is fine, though," I joke, moving slowly to my feet. There aren't many people on the ice tonight, just a few couples and what looks like a family, the adults helping the little ones lace up their skates. Someday, maybe that'll be me, helping my kiddos learn how to ice skate, to enjoy the holidays to the fullest, as my dad taught me.

"What's up?"

"Hmm?" I snap out of my daze, turning to meet Sebastian's gaze.

"You seem distracted. Everything okay?"

"Yeah, yeah." I offer him my hand, and we take to the ice, Sebastian stumbling a bit but staying upright as we join the flow of the rink. "Just thinking about my dad. He loved the holidays. He was so full of life, and so giving."

"Like you."

"What? No, not really. I'm not nearly as selfless as he was." Sebastian squeezes my hand, our gloves preventing our skin from touching, but the sentiment is well meant. "Now, have you ever been ice skating?"

He's moving smoothly now but still hesitant to pick up the

pace. He scoffs at me, his lip curling up in offense. "Please. I probably learned to ice skate before you were walking."

After calculating in my head, I nod. "Okay, maybe. But I was probably crawling. You're only a few years older than me."

"Three years and seven months," he retorts, flashing a smile at me. "Your birthday's in September, right?"

"How do you know that?"

"Apparently, your mom and Phoebe compared our zodiac signs."

"Of course they did. Wait, so your birthday is…"

"In February," we say in unison.

"How are we celebrating?" I ask.

The music fades out and into a different song, and "I'm Dreaming of a White Christmas" echoes around us. First, we danced to it, and now we're skating to it. A shiver that has nothing to do with my temperature runs through my body. We have a first kiss song.

"You're helping me celebrate?" Sebastian pulls me back to our bench after two laps around the ring, where there are thermoses waiting for us. He hands me one, the heat warming through to my skin. Where did they come from? I glance around, expecting to see Mike or someone else sneaking around, but there's no one familiar.

"I love birthdays," I exclaim as we take a seat, inhaling the rich scent of chocolate. "Oh, I love you too."

Sebastian clears his throat, and when I glance over at him, he's watching me with amusement.

"Sorry, the hot chocolate and I were having a moment."

"I noticed. It seems very special." He laughs. "And I'm not at all surprised that you love birthdays. Is there a holiday you don't like?"

He's stumped me now, and as I sip my drink, I rack my brain. "New Year's."

"New Year's? Why?"

"Everyone's always in a rush to get to the next day, the next month, the next year. We need to learn to savor the time we have. You never know when it'll be your last moments with someone."

Sebastian wraps an arm around my shoulders, and I sink into his warmth, hating that I said something so melancholy on our first official date. "Think of it this way. New Year's is also beautiful. You're celebrating that you're here for another year, that you have more time to make the most of."

"I've never thought about it like that, but you're right. For someone who's normally very positive, you'd think I would have made that connection."

I bury my face in Sebastian's neck, enjoying the warmth of his skin against my cheeks.

"Damn, your nose is cold, Angel."

With a chuckle, I press my face into a different spot. Sebastian squirming definitely gives me great pleasure. He sure as hell has made me squirm enough.

In a flash, his hand is on the nape of my neck again, and instead of leading me around the rink, he's bringing my mouth to his. Our lips melt into a sweet, warm kiss, moving together out of instinct and pure need. Without breaking our connection, I take his drink and set it beside me with mine.

His other hand cups my face, deepening our kiss. He sweeps my mouth thoroughly with his tongue, caressing my own with it, and when we break apart, we're both nearly breathless.

"Oh god."

"Yes?" Sebastian smirks, and I swat at him playfully.

"There are kids here," I hiss, glancing around the ice rink.

"Oh, they're too busy falling on their asses to notice us. But if you prefer, we can get out of here." His eyes darken, his insinuation clear, and my ankle agrees. It's been a beautiful evening, but I'm ready to see where the night takes us.

"That sounds perfect." I jerk away, hurrying to untie my skates, and in the process, my elbow brushes something hard... and a warm wetness seeps into my leggings.

Sebastian did a fantastic job of turning me on, but I know I'm not that wet... yet. I glance over slowly, already knowing what happened. "Shit."

"What happened?" Sebastian looks up from his own laces, glancing around me.

"Oh my god." We reach for the cups, setting them upright, and hurry into our shoes as fast as possible. "Well, at least I caught it all," I joke, standing carefully in my soggy leggings.

Way to build the moment, Amber. Jesus.

"We can go to my place here in the city, if you prefer. It's closer than the estate, or your place."

"I won't have anything to change into, Sebastian." We make our way to the car, leaving the beautiful winter wonderland behind.

"For what I have in mind, you don't need anything to change into."

"Oh, hot cocoa covered leggings do it for you, then?" I quip as we stop by the car.

He bursts out laughing, setting the cups on the roof of the car and opening the door for me. "Yes, that's exactly it. I can't resist it. But seriously, you're not wearing those leggings home. You're drenched, and you could catch a cold, or an infection."

Realization dawns on me, and my cheeks flush. I'm thankful for the cover of night and the fact that we're not under a streetlight. "You want me to ride without pants?"

"I do."

"You're serious?"

"I'm dead serious. Leggings off, Amber. Now."

FOURTEEN

Sebastian

ARE YOU HAPPY NOW, MR. STERLING?

Amber's eyes darken, and for a moment, I fear I've angered her, but then she unzips her boots and steps out of them. Her fingers trail the hem of her shirt before pulling it up enough to find the waist of her leggings. She hooks her fingers in the sides, her eyes never wavering from mine as she slips them over her hips. They pool around her ankles, the lace trim of panties impossible to miss.

"Are you happy now, Mr. Sterling?"

I grunt in response, opening the passenger side door for her. She gathers her boots and clothes before climbing in, stretching her top to provide a layer between her bare ass and the leather. I grab her boots and soaked clothes from her arms before shutting the door, reminding myself to breathe as I pop the trunk with my key fob and toss in the clothes. I slam the trunk a bit harder than necessary.

By the time I'm seated in the driver's seat, I've caught my breath and collected my bearings a bit. The engine roars to life, and my hands grip the steering wheel, my knuckles already white as I wheel onto the main road.

At the first stop sign, I glance at Amber out of the corner of my eye, at her milky white thighs exposed in the streetlight. My eyes roam further, to her hands clasped in her lap, her fingers tapping lightly on the top of the opposite hand.

"Cold?" I break the silence, lifting my eyes to hers, and as she opens her mouth, a horn blares from behind us, making us both jump. I refocus on the road; thankfully, my apartment is just a few minutes from here. "I can turn the heat up."

"I'm fine, really."

Recalling the way her clothes slid over her figure, I'd have to agree. While it's obvious there's an attraction between us, I'm not sure how fast this train will be moving. Are we chugging along carefully, or are we charging full steam ahead, all the bells and whistles sounding the alarm?

"Will Giz be okay without you?" After having Amber and Gizmo stay with me for a while, I've learned he has certain expectations out of anyone in his vicinity, but Amber is his favorite person on the planet.

"He should be fine." She reaches to the floorboard for her purse, and she pulls out her phone as I turn into the parking garage. She doesn't have a password on her phone, and many times, she's left it lying around the house. She has nothing to hide, ever, and I can't help but recall Charlotte always being adamant about her phone security.

In hindsight, now I know why, but I never connected all the dots back then. I haven't thought of Charlotte much, minus her surprise visit to my house, but when her name crosses my mind now, my chest doesn't ache. I've begun to realize we weren't well-matched in the first place.

Once I park and cut the ignition, Amber hands me her phone, where a selfie of Ava and Gizmo curled up on the couch proves how happy her fur child is. "See, he's perfectly fine. Now, we have an issue."

"We do?"

"Yes. I have to walk into this building with my ass hanging out. I don't know about you, but I don't go around showing everyone my goodies."

"The elevator goes directly to my front door. We just have to get there." I rack my brain for an idea, glancing around the car and peering into the back seat. Her jacket's soaked, as well, but... nothing I'm wearing got hit by the flood of chocolate.

I hop out of the car, run around the front, and open the door for Amber.

"I told you—"

"Be patient, please." I grab the hem of my sweatshirt and pull it over my head. The cold bites at my skin, but it's not unbearable.

"Tie the sleeves around your waist, and it should cover... your goodies."

As I hand over the shirt, Amber's gaze roams my chest. Her lips part softly, and when her eyes meet mine, I'm no longer chilly at all. Every part of me is aflame, my skin prickling as if a million needles are stabbing me all over.

She steps out and I keep standing in front of her, the door and my body blocking her from anyone that could be in the parking garage. I stare up at the sky as she rearranges herself, the stars illuminating the world around us, and it's overwhelming to think of how big the world is, how many people exist, and Amber and I are here together, by chance.

"Alright, let's go in." She interrupts my pensive thoughts, and I nod in agreement.

"Sounds like a plan."

I offer her my arm, and she takes it, moving out of her safe cocoon and shutting the door easily behind her. I lock the car, and we make our way to the lobby in companionable silence, take the first free elevator, and by the time we're in the penthouse, she's visibly relaxed.

"You seem like you're feeling better already."

"Much. Just a bit sticky," she replies as the door opens.

I can feel her eyes on me as I hang my keys and toss my wallet and phone on the table in the foyer. "Let me run a shower for you. You'll feel much better after that. Make yourself at home."

I motion toward the furniture and the kitchen before heading down the hall to my room and the adjoined bathroom. After rifling through my closet and drawers, I emerge with a shirt and boxers my shopper bought for me, ones that are entirely too small. They might be too small for Amber, though, especially after I've seen her full figure.

Better than nothing, right? *Or is it?*

I should have hired the shopper to bring things for her. What was I thinking? I could kick my own ass for not considering it sooner. I switch on the water in my shower and check the temperature until it's perfect. For me, that is. I don't know how Amber takes a shower, but she can adjust it as she needs.

The bathroom door opens, and she pads across the tile in her sweater dress, a glass of water in one hand and my sweater in the other. I'm still shirtless, and it's impossible to miss her eyes roaming over my chest.

She takes a sip of her water before setting it on the sink. "I found the kitchen, but I couldn't find where you put your dirty laundry."

She waves my sweatshirt around, and I nod toward the corner of the bathroom to my three-compartment laundry basket. She glances in the different sections before tossing it in with the colors and giving me her attention again.

"You don't have any Christmas decorations here, Sebastian." She plants her hands on her hips, narrowing her eyes at me. "This is absolutely unacceptable."

The hem of her dress barely brushes her thighs, and it's a completely unfair advantage. "I haven't even been staying here much," I remind her. "We decorated the house."

"Still. It could use a festive touch."

"If it makes you happy, you can decorate after your shower."

"Oh, you'll allow it? Nice try. I already ordered some shit to be delivered."

"Who the hell did you find to deliver Christmas decorations at ten o'clock at night?"

"Well, it'll be here in the morning," she amends. "But still."

"In the morning?" I step closer to her, tilting my head until my nose brushes his. "Does that mean you plan on staying the night?"

Her quick intake of breath is a straight spark to my dick, and my pants are suddenly much tighter than they felt before. Before I can over think, I cover her mouth with mine and she responds immediately, her lips melting into mine perfectly.

I pull her to me, devouring her mouth as her hands land on my chest, the contact warm and pleasant. Her thumbs each find a nipple, caressing them as she returns my kiss with all her might, and my pants are now so tight that there's no way she can't feel my arousal against her thigh.

Shit. She's still sticky and probably uncomfortable. My hands move of their own accord, pulling her dress over her head and tossing it aside. Reaching around, I unclasp her bra with a quick flick of my wrist, and she lowers her arms, allowing the loops to fall off her and the dainty item to hit the floor. A pang of longing to appreciate her beauty in it hits, but maybe next time. She needs to be clean and comfortable.

"Bash, you don't have to—"

"Shh." I brush away her protests, leading her around the stone wall to the walk-in shower.

She steps under the spray, her body relaxing under the water. I strip out of my jeans and join her, leaving my boxers on. She leans her head back, wetting her hair, and I pump shampoo into my hand and lather it together before massaging it into her scalp.

She's a ragdoll under my touch, her shoulders loose and her neck lolling. After her hair is rinsed, I offer her the body wash before turning my back while she gets clean. The personal aspect of this just hit me, and I don't want to make her uncomfortable. The sounds of her scrubbing her body, her contented sigh as she rinses off, are breathtaking.

I jump when she touches my back, then relax as she rubs slow circles against my skin. Judging by the slickness under her palms, she's putting body wash on me, as well. Her hands travel over my shoulders and down my arms before they disappear.

"I'll get dressed and let you finish up." Her voice is the quietest I've ever heard it, but not in a negative way. She's just comfortable, and that thought makes me happy. More than happy, more like roaring in triumph, but I just nod, reaching to the wall for her towel and passing it without glancing at her.

"Alright, I'm out. It's all yours," she calls, and the next thing I know, the click of the bathroom door closing behind her sounds throughout the room. Hurrying to get myself clean, possibilities run through my mind. It seems as if Amber likes me, and by the way she responds to our physical contact, I'd like to think we share an attraction. I just don't want to make her uncomfortable. If nothing else happens this evening, it would still be perfect.

But if something does, I'm more than okay with that too.

By the time I emerge from the bathroom in gray sweatpants and a loose T-shirt, my hormones have calmed, and my emotions are at ease. The hardwood floors are cold, and as I head into the living room, I make up my mind to turn on the gas fireplace ASAP. Amber has made herself comfy, sitting cross-legged on the couch, and I do a double take at the sight before me. Willow is sprawled out in Amber's lap, head thrown back for the neck scratches being given in abundance.

"Look who I finally got to meet," Amber coos, and Willow meows softly, and quite pitifully, if I'm being honest. "We're best friends now."

"Ironic, as she never likes anyone but me," I tell her. Amber's eyes follow me as I switch on the fireplace and pour myself a glass of Scotch from the decanter on the end table. "Would you like some?"

"No, thank you. I have my water." She nods toward the glass on her side table. "Funny how different our pets are. Gizmo's love can be bought by anyone with treats and ear scratches."

As if aware I've discovered her secret, Willow jumps up, dives off the couch, and shakes her whole body.

"Oh, I see how it is," Amber jokes, nudging the white fluff ball with her foot. Willow takes off, a case of the zoomies settling in, and disappears after a few laps around the room.

A million unsaid things flood through my mind, from another comment about our pets to the random thought of renting a portable ice rink for the gala. But all those things die on my tongue as Amber looks up at me expectantly from the couch.

What is she expecting?

She pats the cushion next to her. "Won't you join me?"

"I..." My voice cracks, and after a quick sip of my drink, I'm prepared to try again. To be brave, to say what I actually want and mean. "Let's go to bed, Amber."

Her lips part, curling up at the edges in a pleased smile. "Let's go to bed, Bash."

I down the last of my drink and set the glass on the table easily before offering Amber my hand. She takes it, and I pull her to her feet, the scent of my body wash on her skin filling my chest with an indescribable feeling. I pull her to me, wrapping my arms around her waist and covering her mouth with mine. I break the kiss, bending to tuck my arm under her knees and picking her up in one swoop.

Her cheeks are pink as I carry her to my room. "At least I'm not injured this time."

"Let's hope for no accidents tonight, shall we? We seem to have had our fair share and more."

"Agreed." She nips at my earlobe, the slight pain exhilarating, and I walk faster, relieved to see my door come into view.

Amber turns the knob, and we reach my bed in a flash, where I lay her down gently. Her hair fans over the pillows, my T-shirt and boxers hugging her just right, and all I can think about is how sweet she tastes. I wonder if she's as sweet between her legs.

Covering my body with hers, I take her lips again, my tongue dancing with hers thoroughly before trailing kisses over her chin and down her neck.

"Amber." My voice is muffled in her neck, but she must hear me, because she responds breathlessly.

"Sebastian."

"I plan to spend the night devouring you, if you have no objections to that."

"On one condition."

"What's that?"

"I get to devour you too."

FIFTEEN

Amber

A NEW SIDE OF HIM

My words are brave, and the way Sebastian relaxes against me after I say them spurs my confidence on. There's nothing sexier than a man that can admit he wants you, but the way Sebastian says he wants to devour me is somehow different. Primal.

It's a new side of him, one I'm more than willing to get to know. He continues worshiping my body for a moment, his lips nipping and kissing my neck, before sitting up and straddling my legs.

When he pulls my shirt between his hands, the tearing of the fabric echoing around the room with a shriek, it feels like I'll never breathe right again. I lie before him, my chest exposed and my nipples pebbled and eager for the attention my neck just received. His eyes roam over my body as if I'm made of gold, as if I'm some priceless treasure, and when he takes my nipple into his mouth, I cry out in pleasure and something else, an emotion throbbing in my chest that isn't just lust.

He peppers kisses over my stomach and just above the waist of his boxers, looking up at me with the excitement I normally reserve for Christmas trees and ice skating. I suppose this is like unwrapping a present, though.

He slides his fingers into the waist of the underwear before pulling them down until I can kick my feet out. He presses my knees apart until I'm spread before him, exposed. But I'm not self-conscious.

That same emotion still throbs in my chest as he dives between my legs, eyes closed as if he's just tasted the best thing in the world. He licks and sucks, his tongue swirling around the perfect spot, and my hands find his hair, tangling in it of their own accord, and when he groans against me, the vibration sends me over the edge, spiraling into an oblivion of pleasure, where there's just me and Sebastian and his amazing fucking mouth.

When the feeling returns to my legs, I sit up, swinging them under me as Sebastian starts to climb on the bed.

"Wait," I command, my hand on his chest, and he obeys but watches me curiously. "I told you I had conditions."

Sebastian moves to his feet, his cheeks a brilliant red.

"Mr. Sterling, are you blushing?" I prop up on my knees, running my hands over his smooth chest, brushing over his nipples a few times for good measure. "These look a little tight."

I struggle with the strings of his sweatpants, and finally, he covers his hands with mine, our eyes locked as he unties them, the only sound is our heavy breathing. He pushes them to the floor, his dick springing free to meet me eye to eye.

And holy shit, Sebastian Sterling is sporting a thick member. The thought of him filling me to the brim, the sensation of being stretched so real in my mind that I can practically feel it, has me clenching my thighs in anticipation.

"You don't have to—"

Before Sebastian can finish his statement, I take him into

my mouth, relaxing my jaw and making a fist with my left hand like I read in a magazine in high school. Does it work? I don't know. But in my mind, it does, and I never gag when doing it.

My enthusiastic attack has me gagging, so I back off a bit but keep sucking, one hand moving to cup Sebastian's balls and the other to grasp the base of his cock. He thrusts his hips gently as I suck and fondle, as if he's afraid he'll hurt me or make me gag.

"You okay?"

His palm cups my cheek, and I hum, "Mm-hmm," without stopping.

His groan sends a thrill through me, and he throws his head back in reckless abandon, his hips moving faster and faster, lost in the pleasure I'm giving him. Exhilaration floods me at the power, the realization that I'm doing this, making this man lose all self-control. His balls tighten in my palm, and his hand finds my shoulder, a warning for what's about to come.

Pun intended.

As the warmth hits the back of my throat, our eyes meet, his hand tightening on my shoulder. The rest of the world fades away, and when his body stills, he releases a heavy breath before pulling me into his arms and covering my mouth with his.

He lays me gently on the bed, covering my body with his without breaking our kiss, the taste of our pleasure mixed together. Something warm and hard brushes against my thigh, and I open my legs and wrap them around his waist. Sebastian stops, seemingly searching my eyes for consent, and I answer by pulling his lips back to mine, allowing them to mold together again as he presses against my entrance, his cock throbbing. I'm more than ready for him, and he slides into me slowly.

"Fuck, you're perfect," he mutters against my mouth, and my teeth grab his bottom lip teasingly. Our mouths are a tangled mess of lips and teeth and sucking as he thrusts into me. He grasps my waist, securing me in place, and if it didn't feel so damn good, I'd be embarrassed by the moan he pulls from me with his movements.

I'm dizzy with emotions and arousal as he gives me every inch of him, his mouth moving to my neck to nibble and kiss. I tighten my legs around him, and he's so deep inside me, I wonder if he can feel my soul pulsing.

He thrusts harder and faster, sitting up but leaving his hands around my waist. He stares down at me with wild eyes. I tweak my nipples, one hand on each breast, and his eyes widen as he pauses for a moment.

"You like that?" I ask. "When I touch my nipples?"

Sebastian nods, his movements slower but still hard as hell, and it's absolute perfection. He hits the spot just right, and with his next movement and my nipple tweaking, I'm over the edge before I can catch my breath.

He follows closely behind, his body tensing then relaxing with a low growl I feel to my core. He rolls onto the bed beside me and pulls me close for a chaste kiss. Afterward, I bury my face in his chest, my body more satisfied than I can ever recall it being. My heart, though, is a little on edge. But I'll worry about that later. For now, I want to enjoy this moment, this feeling.

"I could lie here and listen to your heart beat all night." My words are honest, embarrassingly so. "I know that sounds creepy."

"It's not creepy." His chest vibrates with the deepness of his voice, his emotions shining through his tone. "It's... sweet. It makes me feel."

"Feel what?"

"Everything, Amber. Everything."

He pulls me closer, pressing a kiss to the top of my head,

and my heart does that weird thing again that has nothing to do with the mind-blowing orgasms. No, it's more than that.

"I'm going to freshen up. I'll be right back." I disentangle myself from his limbs, shooting him a smile before climbing out of bed, pulling his shirt over my head, and heading to the bathroom. After relieving myself, I wash my hands and face, then rinse my mouth with mouthwash. I feel better, but my mind is still running at full speed.

I don't have my life together. I've been jumping from one job to the next since I became an adult, and until three weeks ago, I never knew if I would make my rent. How am I going to do this with Sebastian Sterling, mega millionaire and king of having his shit together?

Staring in the mirror, I take in every aspect of my appearance. My just-fucked hair, the smattering of freckles that lingers on my nose year-round, and my body still flushed from our passion. Maybe it's time I consider getting a real career of some sort. Perhaps I should give up on my party planning dream and do something concrete and dependable.

In my heart, I know I can't do that. I've never been one to live a lie, and I don't want to start now, especially if that decision is influenced by a man.

A man I've only slept with once. Good lord, what am I thinking? This must be that post-sex haze I've heard of. Sebastian already knocked me loopy.

I rinse my mouth again before glancing one more time in the mirror, the hesitation and doubt that was in my eyes earlier replaced by something else.

Hope.

Because if my dad taught me nothing else, he taught me how to persevere.

Sebastian groans, his face tucked into my neck. "The last thing I want to do is get out of this bed."

The sun shines through the open curtains, and I'm fleetingly glad we're at the top of the damn building, otherwise our antics last night could have been available to anyone walking by.

"Let's not, then. We can just stay here all day. Order food and take the day off."

"While that sounds heavenly, it wouldn't be wise." Sebastian chuckles before pressing his lips to my neck. He trails pecks up my jaw, and I turn to let him kiss my mouth softly.

"Why's that?"

"The party is tomorrow," he whispers against my mouth before kissing me again, my lips instinctively responding. Something in his words sends alarms throughout my body, but I push them aside and focus on the feel of his lips on mine, his hands burning into my skin as they caress my stomach and chest.

"Oh."

"Oh, what?" He dives back into my neck, his lips leaving a torturous trail to my breasts.

"Tomorrow. The gala's tomorrow," I squeak out, my head rolling back in ecstasy as he takes a nipple into his mouth. "We have so much to do. And we've got to get to the house. My mom will be there cooking today."

"Mm-hmm," Sebastian mumbles against my breast, still licking and sucking the pink peaks. His hand snakes between my legs, finding my clit like it's second nature, the circular movements as heavenly as his kisses. "We have time."

I open my mouth to object, but the words that come out change from what my brain planned on saying. "Okay."

As if he'd been holding back the last of his reserve, Sebastian cups me completely, his thumb resuming the circular motions, and my hips move against his skin, hungry for what's building within me. A finger teases my entrance, barely moving in and out of me as his thumb continues its dance, and as he moves faster and faster, the pressure builds within me. I close my eyes and Sebastian grips my chin, tilting my head toward him.

"Oh no, Angel. I want to watch your face while you come." His words send me over the edge, warmth flooding through me as my body quakes beneath his touch, our eyes locked.

I'm still recovering from the aftershock when Sebastian gathers me up, flips me onto my hands and knees faster than you can say Holly Jolly Christmas, and something hard and wet presses against me from behind, trailing over my ass cheeks and down to rub my swollen clit. The sensations shock me and my leg twitches, my body anticipating when he will—

"Oh, fuck," I hiss, clenching the pillow with both fists as he slams into me from behind, my body stretching to accommodate his girth.

He slowly rocks into me, hands gripping my waist, and while last night was sweet and passionate, this is about more than that. It's about craving, and I love every moment of him taking me from behind. He moves faster and faster, his balls slapping my ass as he gives me everything he's got.

My nipples brush against the covers, heightening my arousal, and my hand slips between my thighs to find my clit as he pumps into me so hard the bed knocks against the wall. Just as his body stiffens, I explode, too, my body clenching around him and milking every last drop.

SIXTEEN

Sebastian

I THINK SHE'S LOST HER MIND

"Was traffic bad?" Amber's mom greets me with a one-armed hug, her eyes wide with concern. "I thought you'd be here an hour ago."

"It was a bit rough, Joy. Sorry we kept you waiting." I'm not lying, the roads were more crowded than I anticipated. But no, being late was worth it.

Every moment I spend touching Amber makes me want a million more. Even now, as she scrolls through the notes on her phone, I wonder if her thighs are sore, if her neck smells like me. The idea of marking her as mine gives me immense pleasure.

"Bash?" Joy's staring me down again, eyebrows furrowed.

"I'm sorry, I was in another world." *In bed with her daughter. Straighten up, Sebastian.* "What did you say?"

"I think I've got all the food ready. No pineapples, though." She shoots me a withering look as I follow her into the kitchen. "We don't need another reaction, especially in the middle of this party."

"Yes, ma'am," I agree. "Although it was delicious, I have to admit." We enter the kitchen, and the transformation gobsmacks me.

There are at least ten people I don't know bustling around the area, carrying platters and setting up different arrangements. One girl is making a fruit bouquet, and it's absolutely gorgeous, but of course, none of my favorite fruit.

"I have no doubt. That doesn't mean we're risking it, though." She shakes her finger at me.

"Where did all these people come from?"

"Hmm? Oh, Amber hired them. They'll be serving, setting up, helping to decorate, and anything else we've forgotten."

When in the hell did she have time to hire people? She sprained her ankle and has been taking me on Christmas outings. What is she, Superwoman? Is she changing in a phone booth somewhere in between activities?

The doorbell rings, interrupting my thoughts, and I make my way back to the front door to see who's arrived.

"Hey, Bash," Junior exclaims as soon as I open the door. His wife, Faye, is curled into his side, her teeth chattering.

"Hey, guys, come on in." I step back and motion them inside. "How are you? How's the tree farm?"

"Oh, we're great. Word got out that Sebastian Sterling bought a bunch of trees from us, and we're sold out of everything now."

"That's great news! And surprising. How did everyone know?"

Faye unravels her scarf from around her neck and hangs it on the coat rack. "Amber posted about us on the social media pages she's running for the event."

"Oh, right." I nod, although I haven't the foggiest idea what Amber's been posting on social media.

"There you are!" Amber's squeal startles all three of us, and I'm even more startled when she runs up and hugs Junior, then

Faye, smiling widely at them. "I'm so glad you guys could make it. It's going to be the best night."

"What exactly are we doing tonight?" I question her, but she avoids my gaze, still focused on our guests.

"Is Rachel coming?" Amber asks.

"She'll be here in a bit," Faye tells her. "She had a few errands to run."

"Let me show you to the kitchen. You can meet my mom."

I'm about to follow them when the doorbell rings again. I open the door and find myself face to face with Herschel, and I have to say, it does grind my gears a bit.

"Herschel." I clear my throat, crossing my arms as our eyes meet.

"Bash. You have to know I didn't give Charlotte the key. She's been going through my things. I cut her off, so then she stole things from me to pawn." He throws his hands into the air. "I think she's lost her mind. I told her she's no longer welcome in my home. She can't be trusted."

My heart softens toward the old man, and I step back to let him in. "Well, I know how she can be, and that's low, even for Charlotte." We shake hands, an unspoken truce passing between us, and he steps in and shuts the door behind him.

"What are you doing here, anyway?"

"Oh, your woman called me. Mike's parking outside. She invited him too." His eyes are as wide as saucers, the idea of socializing with the staff evidently foreign to him.

"She did, did she?" What in the world is this woman up to? "Alright. Well, let's head into the—"

The doorbell rings again, and at this point, I'm expecting Santa Claus himself. "You go on through. Apparently, I'm the door greeter this afternoon."

Herschel shuffles off, and I reach for the door once more.

"Hey, Mr. Sterling." Mike stands awkwardly at the threshold.

"Come on in, Mike. How are you this afternoon?"

"I'm just fine, thank you. Amber insisted I come," he explains, and I wave him on through.

"Head that way. The mastermind is somewhere, no doubt plotting something else."

I didn't even shut the door after Mike, and it's a good thing, because coming up the steps is a crowd of people.

Phoebe and Ava, I know, but the third woman chattering with them is someone I've never seen before. Ava has Gizmo wrapped in a blanket in her arms, and he doesn't look pleased.

"Hey, Sebastian." Ava smiles as they all wipe their feet. "This is Rachel. Her grandparents are evidently here, as well."

"So you're the famous Rachel." I laugh. "Your grandfather is convinced that Amber should know you from somewhere."

Ava glances between Rachel and me, her nose wrinkled. "Now that you mention it, you do look familiar, Rachel."

Rachel shrugs, but I notice the way she looks to the side when replying. "I'm not sure."

"I wonder if this is everyone," Phoebe interjects, glancing at me over Rachel's and Ava's heads.

"I didn't even know any of you were coming, so I don't know who is missing."

"Okay, who's here?" Ava questions me, and I get how she could be intimidating in court. She doesn't blink and her face doesn't move an inch as she awaits my response.

"You three, Junior and Faye, Mike and Herschel, Amber, Joy, and like ten people I don't know are apparently here to serve at the party tomorrow and do anything else we deem necessary," I rattle off. "Think it's safe for me to stop manning the door?"

"I think so, for now," Phoebe says, so I lock the door behind them and help them hang their coats and scarves. We head into the sitting room to find everyone piled around in various positions, some sitting on the floor and a few leaning against walls.

Amber is seated on the couch, her face shining up at me brightly.

"What in the world is going on?" I finally break the silence, smiling at the echo of laughter around the room. "Why are all these people here?"

Not that I mind, really. These are all people I can tolerate, but an ideal afternoon and evening would be spent alone with Amber.

Amber claps her hands together, still smiling so widely and brightly that I wonder if my eyes will be able to take much more. She's so beautiful. I feel unworthy.

"It's Christmas movie night!" she exclaims, pointing above the fireplace. Sure enough, a projector screen is unrolling as we speak, and after glancing around, I find the projector mounted at a perilous looking height.

"How did you—"

"You may not want to know," she interrupts. "But my ankle survived, and that's all that matters."

Junior chuckles from his spot beside his wife on the love seat. "You better keep watch on yourself, girl. Bash may not be able to get to you as fast if he's at work or something."

It hits me then, how temporary Amber and I are supposed to be. Sure, we're no longer "fake," but we haven't had a real conversation about what this is between us, and after tomorrow, she has no reason to deal with me anymore.

"Alright." Amber claps her hands together gleefully. "Welcome, everyone, to our first Christmas movie night." Her words aren't lost on me. Our *first*. My heart is beating so wildly, it pulses in my throat. That means she anticipates more of them.

"We're going to watch *Christmas Vacation*, and we have

some special treats prepared for you guys to enjoy while we watch."

At her words, the servers emerge from the kitchen door, each of them carrying a tray, or napkins, or something else we may need. One has a cooler of bottled water.

They set down their wooden platters to reveal they're covered with peppermint, marshmallows, candies, sprinkles, and any other kind of topping you could imagine.

"We're having hot cocoa charcuterie boards while we watch!" Amber proclaims.

Everyone makes appreciative sounds or comments, and before I know it, we're all drinking unique blends of hot cocoa and settling in to watch the movie. About halfway through, I glance around at the faces of people close to me or Amber or who have been part of this journey together.

I consider the possibility that I have something in my life I haven't wanted in a long time.

I, Sebastian Sterling, could have friends.

SEVENTEEN

Sebastian

I'M NOT OLD, I JUST APPRECIATE SLEEP

"Have a good night. Thanks for coming," Amber calls to our guests as they make their way down the front walk. I slip my arms around her waist from behind and press my lips to her cheek.

"I hope you had a fun night." She spins in my arms, her hands interlocking behind my head, and the normalcy of the whole thing makes it hard for me to swallow.

"I did. It was amazing," I reassure her when I regain my voice, pulling her flush against me. "However, I don't know how you've had time to plan everything you've been doing."

"What are you talking about? I haven't done that much."

She moves out of my arms to lock up the house, and my hands tighten and then release, trying to resist the temptation to touch her again.

"You're amazing, Angel. The party and all the Christmas activities on top of that. Hiring people, managing social media."

"Don't be ridiculous. Now you, sir, need to go get ready."

"Ready for what? It's ten o'clock at night."

"How old are you again?" she teases me, her eyes glinting playfully.

"I'm not old. I just appreciate sleep."

"Oh, is that all we're doing tonight, then? Sleeping?" Her voice softens to a low murmur, her insinuation clear as day, and as she sashays into the living room, I heed her orders, rushing to our bedroom as fast as I can.

Our bedroom. What has this woman done to me?

Laid across the bed is what I assume Amber wants me to wear, but I'm not sure I can pull it off. There's very little material, though, and while she's seen me in all my glory, there's something personal about appearing half-dressed before someone.

The shorts are soft and velvety, and the image of Amber running her hands across them... while I'm wearing them... is enough to spur me on. I'm out of my jeans and T-shirt in a flash and start pulling the shorts up and securing them around my waist with the belt. There's no shirt, just the signature red hat with a soft white poof at the end.

Last but not least is a small red bag, but it's tied shut, and I'm not sure if she means for me to open it now or when we're together.

Speaking of, is she ever coming in here? I throw the bag over my shoulder and make my way through the house. She's not in the kitchen, but the lights are still dimmed in the living room. Surely she didn't fall asleep on me.

"Ho, ho, ho." I announce my presence as I enter the room, glancing around for her. The furniture is empty, the whole room quiet except for the ticking of the clock. Anticipation builds inside me, the chase arousing me more than I'd admit out loud. Amber's always been playful, but our intimacy has just gotten started, so seeing what else she's up for is exciting.

Turning on my heel, I survey the room. The only light is

the Christmas tree, and beside it is a package wrapped in glittery red paper and tied up with a green bow. How the hell did she get it in here?

"I thought I was the one bringing the package tonight," I mutter.

Her laughter's muffled, but still I drop my sack on the floor beside the box and reach for the ribbon. The silkiness slides between my fingers and falls to the ground, and then I slip my thumb between the folds of the paper, tearing it slowly. Eventually, the paper falls to the floor, as well, and then Amber is pushing the lid up, rising to her feet and stepping out of the box with a sultry smile. How in the hell did she fold up to fit in there?

"Your present has arrived, Mr. Sterling."

She's wearing that fucking elf costume from the first day we met. A few changes have been made, though. She's not wearing the leggings, just the top, her ass cheeks peeking out from the hem of the top. Her hair flows freely around her shoulders, and the hat is crooked on her head. The lights from the tree reflect in her eyes.

She flattens her palms against my chest and pushes lightly. Following her lead, I let her guide me backward to the couch, those damn shoes jingling with each step she takes. The cushions hit the back of my knees, and I sink into the velvet, holding my breath as I watch Amber, waiting to see what her next move will be.

"You lost something." She holds up my red bag, swaying it back and forth in front of me.

I didn't even see her grab it, but then again, I've been distracted. "I wasn't sure if I should open it yet."

"Go ahead. Open it." I take it from her, pulling at the string slowly until the bag opens, and I stretch it further to fit my hand inside. I clasp my hand around something warm and hard. A container of some kind. When I pull it out and read the label, I can't help but chuckle.

"Hot-chocolate-flavored body paint," I murmur, watching Amber shift back and forth, almost as if she's nervous. "There's someone I know that loves hot cocoa."

"Who could that be?" She sinks to her knees, bracing her arms on my thighs. She takes the jar from me and opens it easily before dipping her finger inside. The moment her finger touches her lips, she sighs, and that one small sound nearly undoes me. My shorts twitch between us as she sucks her finger into her mouth, and the memory of her warm, welcoming throat combined with the sight of her lapping up the chocolate is trying my patience, but I behave.

"See what else is in your bag of treats," she demands, licking a stray bit of chocolate from the corner of her mouth. I obey immediately, pulling out a paintbrush, and she takes it before I can comment. She swirls it into the container and dives into her work with a serious expression. She draws over my chest, dipping the brush back in occasionally to replenish her paint.

Then she pulls at the waist of my shorts, and I lift so she can pull them down all the way, my dick springing free between us. She inhales quickly, her eyes roaming over my body, taking in her own artwork, before she adds a few strokes to my inner thighs. The chocolate is warm, not hot, but I'm afraid it's going to harden soon.

Thankfully, she sets her materials aside and climbs onto the couch beside me, propping up on her knees again, and as she lowers her mouth to my chest, I refuse to blink. I don't want to miss a moment of this magical night, of this magical woman that looks at me like I hung the stars in the sky.

Her tongue traces over the chocolate trail she left, lapping and sucking her way across my chest with enthusiasm. The sensation is indescribable, her worshiping my body and her perky ass hovering within arm's reach, the hem of her shirt rising up just enough to show off her cheeks. I can't resist the temptation anymore, and I stretch my arm around her to massage her ass gently, the thrill of it filling my palm and more satisfying my urges.

Amber groans appreciatively, her mouth now trailing around my hips. She glances up at me, her bottom lip tucked between her teeth. She hasn't even touched my dick yet, and it feels like I might explode.

"Is this okay?" Her confidence wavers. I could see it in her eyes even if she hadn't asked, and I hate that she feels less than right now.

"This is more than okay." I bring my other hand to her face, cupping her cheek. "This is perfect. Beyond anything I could imagine."

"Really?"

"Really. And while I'm enjoying every moment of this, what makes it the best is that I'm with you."

She leans into my hand with her eyes closed for a moment, and my thumb caresses her cheekbone. My other hand is still on her ass, but I keep it as still as possible.

Her eyes flash open then, and before I can say another word, she turns her head, taking me into her mouth in a flash. I swallow, forgetting everything I was about to say, and watch Amber take every inch of me into her mouth.

She gags for a moment and backs off, her tongue trailing the tip as her hand moves to grasp me, pumping enthusiastically. Her fucking shoes jingle as she shifts, and I release her ass so I can reach down to rip them off her feet. It gives me immense pleasure to throw them down. It's almost as enjoyable as Amber's mouth and hand on my dick, where she pumps and sucks without stopping.

"Fuck, Amber," I breathe, watching her work her magic. "You're literal perfection."

She glances back at me with a smile, her lips still against my dick, and she pumps harder and harder, her lips teasing me. Something about my dick on her lips, the image of her rubbing me on her face, sends me over the edge, and I explode. My cum coats her mouth and chin in spurts, and it's a fucking majestic sight.

"Damn. Hang on a second." I sit up carefully, fumbling for the shorts I had on earlier, and use the hem to wipe her face clean.

"So, that's something I've never done before," I admit as she curls into my side, our hands intertwining on my chest.

"What, get blown by an elf?"

"Well, obviously that." I laugh. "But no, the face thing."

"Did you not like it?"

"Oh, on the contrary, I liked it very much. It was just a new experience." I move our hands toward her, then lift her chin and cover her mouth with mine.

The taste of me and chocolate on her tongue is tangy and sweet and hot as fuck, and now I want nothing more than to bring her pleasure. I kiss her harder, pressing against her body until she's lying on the couch. I throw one of her legs on the back of the couch, and the other dangles to the floor. Her hair is everywhere, and she lost her hat some time ago.

I grab the chocolate and the paintbrush, then stop with the brush poised over one of Amber's nipples as our eyes lock. "Now it's time for your present. Be a good girl, and you might get more than one."

She whimpers, and I'm glad I already came, because it might have been my undoing. I dive into my own masterpiece, determined to give her the best orgasms of her life tonight.

EIGHTEEN

Amber

CHOCOLATE DOESN'T TASTE THE SAME ALONE

"Girl, you're absolutely glowing." Ava pinches my cheeks, our faces so close I can see the tired lines underneath her eyes. "What has this man done to you?"

"I don't even know," I admit, sipping my hot cocoa. We decided to meet for lunch before setting up everything for the gala tonight. "It seems like it's gone so fast, but then at the same time, it's like I've known him forever."

Ava leans back in her chair, and I can feel her gaze roaming over me, but I ignore it and pick at my chocolate croissant. The icing reminds me of the spirals and stars Sebastian painted on me last night before devouring me, and my cheeks flush of their own accord.

"Uh-huh. You've got it bad, Bambi."

"Enough about me. Let's talk about you. We haven't really hung out in ages."

"This case is killing me." She sighs. "It's like, one minute we make huge progress, then something else appears, and it's two steps back again."

"Maybe one day you can tell me who it is."

"Don't get me started." She rolls her eyes. "They're quite annoying, really. Did Sebastian like the movie night?"

"Yes." I answer a bit too quickly perhaps, but oh well. "He seemed to enjoy the company. An odd grouping, but it turned out well."

"I thought so," Ava agrees, and then I see what she's done, turning the conversation back to me. My best friend is the queen of avoiding talking about her feelings, but this is definitely more than that. She's deliberately doing it.

"Everything ready for tonight?"

"I believe so. If not, it must mean we didn't need it after all." I drain the last of my drink, pushing the rest of my croissant toward Ava. "Here, take this for a snack. I'm full."

Chocolate doesn't taste the same alone, not after licking it off Sebastian's body.

Ava's phone ringing interrupts my memories of the night before, and she groans. "I have to take this."

"Go ahead, I'll get the trash and grab us a drink for the road."

She nods, already putting the phone to her ear, and after throwing away our cups, I make my way to the counter and order another hot cocoa for me and a caramel macchiato for Ava. We've drunk the same drinks for as long as I can remember. It's a nice familiarity to have breakfast with her again, a normalcy I've missed.

After the gala, things will go back to normal for the most part. There will be no need for me to stay with Sebastian, and really, we need to have a discussion. We need to talk about what we're doing, what's real and what's not. Because to me, everything feels more real by the day, and while I think he's on the same page, I don't want a rude awakening.

"Here are your drinks, ma'am."

"Thank you." I smile at the barista, taking one in each hand and heading back to Ava.

She's deep in conversation, and as I come up behind her, I can tell she's angry. She's using her talking-through-her-teeth voice.

"I meant what I said, asshole. Now leave me alone." She drops her phone into her purse with a huff, and I'm wondering whose ass I need to kick.

"What the hell was that?"

She starts at my words, grabbing her purse and jumping up from her chair.

"Just this case." She shakes her head at me before reaching for her drink. "It'll be fine. Let's get going. We've got a party to get ready for." She takes a sip before leading the way to the door.

As we step out into the cold morning air, I sip my drink and nearly spit it all over the place. Ava is drinking hot cocoa like there's no tomorrow, completely oblivious it's the wrong drink. Something is definitely going on, and once this party is over, I'm going to find out what's got her so distracted.

The drive to Bash's estate seems to take no time at all, and as I park in my usual spot, I'm worrying over everything about tonight—all the activities planned for the kids, keeping up with all of Bash's investors and their dates. A sinking feeling in my stomach reminds me that I'm not from his world, and everything I planned for this event is from my world. They may think it's not fancy enough, or the food isn't up to their standards. If they insult my mom's cooking, there will be hell to pay. I won't let anyone talk shit to or about her. With a deep breath, I get out of the car and make my way to the back yard to double-check all of the decorations back there.

To my complete surprise, there's something new and very large in the midst of the decorated trees I bought from the tree farm. A portable ice skating rink has been set up, and I know just who did it.

He strolls down the walk, hands tucked into his pockets and a sheepish smile pulling at his lips. "I hope it's not too much. I just know you love it, and I wanted there to be something for you at this party too."

"Oh, it's perfect." I run and jump into his arms, relieved that he catches me, his hands cupping my ass. I take his face in my hands and kiss him fiercely before letting my legs slide down, but he keeps his arms around me as my feet hit the ground.

"What a greeting. A man could get used to this." We fall in step, his arm still around my shoulders, and head into the house.

"Everything is perfect," I say, taking in the sight of my vision coming to life. "It turned out exactly how I pictured it."

"You did amazing. You make it seem easy too. You've been so calm the whole time."

"Eh, that's just because I have a good poker face." I laugh just as my mom comes bustling around the corner in her gingerbread man apron.

"There you are. I wanted to double-check with you on the desserts and make sure you think everything looks okay."

"Oh, Mom." I take her hands in mine and squeeze. "You know everything you made is perfect. Just breathe."

She obeys me, inhaling and then exhaling slowly.

"They're going to love your delicious food, Joy," Sebastian reassures her. "I could eat your cooking every day for the rest of my life and not get tired of it."

"You're too kind. We could make that happen," she quips, and I don't miss the glance she throws between Sebastian and me.

After giving her a pointed look, I change the subject. "I

suppose we better get ready." I'm in jeans and a T-shirt, and while a lot of this event is more low-key than it's ever been, the dress code is still formal. So, I suppose I should stick to that.

"I'll meet you back here in a little while, then." Sebastian presses a kiss to my temple, and I breathe in his scent, a mixture of mint and laundry detergent. Which is also what I probably smell like, because I've been washing my clothes here and using his toothpaste. His body has claimed me, but the idea of his scent marking me is enough to bring me to my knees.

Clearing my throat, I escape to the room I sleep in and close the door behind me before flipping the lock. Leaning against the wood, I close my eyes and remind myself to breathe. The event is going to be fine, the investors will be happy, and Bash will be delighted. It's a win-win-win situation.

But will I be happy when it's over? I'll go back to working retail and watching Buffy with Gizmo every night.

Not that I don't love that second part, I do, but I'm going to miss what has been my life for three weeks.

After collecting myself, I head to the closet and pull out the garment bag, ready to put on the dress I bought the first day I visited this house after Sebastian asked me to be his fake girlfriend. Before I officially decided to. Sometimes it feels like a million years ago, and then it hits me that it hasn't been long at all.

The red silk slides over my skin, fitting to my body like a glove, and while the front of the dress stops right above my knees, the train trails the floor as I walk over to the closet to find my heels. They're not stilettos—I would definitely sprain my ankle again—but they'll give me a little height and will hopefully make my ass look nice in this dress that Phoebe and my mother talked me into.

What was I thinking?

Maybe I should change.

There's a knock on the door then, and I'm not even done getting ready. Sebastian should know I still need to do my hair and makeup. I crack open the door enough to peep out, but to my relief, it's Ava.

I open the door to let her in and then lock it again.

"I thought you might want some help with your hair and makeup," she offers, glancing around the room. "Oh, wow. This is amazing! Our whole apartment would fit in here."

"Right? It's insane how much room one person can have." I carefully take a seat at the vanity. "Alright, girl. Work your magic."

"Your wish is my command, Cinderella."

NINETEEN

Sebastian

THE WOMAN OF THE HOUR

"This is splendid, Bash. Really. Your little lady has outdone herself." Herschel thumps me on the back, his force quite strong for the old man he appears to be.

"She is something special." I paste on a grin, wondering where the object of our conversation is. Everyone and their mother has arrived, but Amber has yet to appear. She went to get dressed over an hour ago, but maybe something is going on. Maybe she got caught up or had a malfunction. Fuck, if I knew where my phone was, I'd call her, but in the business of getting the party going, it's disappeared.

When Amber told me about most of the plans for the party, I agreed to whatever she suggested, but I didn't realize how homey and comfortable this event would be. Everyone is dressed formally, but the atmosphere is so much different. Having everyone's families here might have something to do with that, as well. Here are kids running and squealing, the ice rink is full of skaters, and all around, it's just... nice.

I've never considered the estate home or even my apartment home. I literally call them the estate or the apartment. But for the first time in forever, this is home. And I like it... I like it a lot. Amber's touch on the place has opened up my heart and made me realize why I love this place. I'm considering moving here again.

I sense her presence before I see her, the warmth of her hand as she slips it into mine. My body turns toward her instinctively, and my god, I'm grateful for the gift of sight. Amber's dress is strapless, the red silk clinging to every mountain and valley of her figure. The hem trails just above her thighs, but the train of the dress touches the ground. The fabric shimmers in the candlelight of the room. Her lips match the dress, a brilliant shade, and suddenly, my pants feel much tighter than they were a few moments ago. Her hair is twisted into an updo, and she's a goddess. But her lips are pinched a bit, her eyes narrowed, and as she squeezes my hand even tighter, I worry that she's nervous.

"Everything okay?" I lean in, whispering in her ear. "I was worried about you."

"Yeah, everything's fine. Ava was talking as she did my hair and makeup, and we got distracted. Sorry I'm late. I wasn't here to greet everyone."

"Oh, it's fine. It's been very low-key."

"Is that okay?"

"It is. It's been the most enjoyable event I've ever attended, if I'm being honest."

Her face lights up, her features relaxing, and while I was being completely honest, I'm also pleased to see her relieved.

"There's the woman of the hour," Herschel bellows, offering a hand to Amber. "This has been the best night, Amber. Thank you for taking care of things, and of my boy here."

Amber takes his hand, her other still wrapped firmly in mine. Herschel insulted Amber on their first meeting, and she won't have forgotten that, but maybe he can make amends and keep his tongue in cheek now. "I'm glad you're enjoying yourself."

She doesn't smile, though, her face friendly but commanding the conversation. God, she's beautiful. She's amazing, and she's mine.

Well, I think she is. I want her to be.

"Herschel, we better do some rounds. You know how that goes." I squeeze Amber's hand, bidding my old friend goodbye, and Amber leads me through the crowd. We stop and talk to several of my investors, and Amber charms their pants off with the story about her ankle incident and discussing her mom's recipes with everyone. By the time we reach the door to the kitchen, I think she's won everyone over—and in one case, even a board member's mother.

"Hey, you two. You're supposed to be partying!" Joy greets us as we duck into the kitchen. The only other people around are servers.

"I needed to get out of that crowd for a moment," I confess, grabbing a glass and heading to the fridge for ice and water from the dispenser. "How's it going in here?"

"It's been a dream. Everything's working out perfectly. I'm just about to start cleaning up."

"No, you are not," Amber says. "I've hired people specifically for cleanup. You are going home, putting your feet up, and watching *A Charlie Brown Christmas*."

"Oh, that sounds heavenly." Joy smiles, the wistfulness in her voice piquing my curiosity.

"It's a tradition. My mom and dad always watched it on Christmas Eve," Amber explains. "Mom and I still watch it every year in honor of him."

"You guys should watch it here, then," I offer, then realize I could be overstepping. And while I had hoped Amber would spend the night with me, I would never suggest it now. She should stick to her traditions with her mom. Hopefully, we'll have our own traditions now.

They exchange a glance before Joy sidles over to me and covers my arm. "That's such a sweet offer, but you two kids have some partying to do yet. I'll be just fine. I may head out shortly and get started on the tradition."

She pats my arm. "You just take good care of my girl, okay?"

"Yes, ma'am."

"Good night, sweetheart." Joy kisses Amber's cheek. "I'll talk to you tomorrow."

"Tonight," Amber insists. "Text me when you get home, please."

Oh, shit. The thought of texts reminds me I've yet to find my phone. Mentally retracing my steps, I set off to scour the house. Damn, why did I put it on silent?

"I'll be back in a minute," I call over my shoulder to Amber. I wanted to take some pictures together. Damn. I might even set one as my background. Then I can look at her in that beautiful dress with her sexy lipstick every day. On second thought, maybe that's not the best idea. I'll never get anything done.

I know it has to be on the first floor, because I haven't been upstairs in ages. Finally, I'm in the foyer, and there it is, on the entrance table. Breathing a sigh of relief, I grab it and swipe through my notifications. I have a text from an unsaved number, but it seems kind of familiar. I can't recall where I've seen the number before, though.

Got them.

That's all it says. Weird. Maybe they texted the wrong number. Without another thought, I tuck my phone into my pocket and head back to the kitchen to find Amber. I'm hoping we can grab a few laps around the ice rink before the night ends.

I find her in the kitchen on a stool, and all of the staff have left. She's nursing a steaming mug of what I'm sure is hot cocoa, and for the first time tonight, she seems tired. I take the mug from her and set it on the counter before wrapping her in my arms. She sinks into my body—we fit together perfectly—and the sigh she releases seems to be filled with tons of worry and exhaustion.

"Feel better now?"

"You have no idea," she mumbles against my chest. My hands move up her back, massaging gently. She moans softly. "That feels so good."

"Oh, does it?"

"Better than sex, maybe."

I burst out laughing, my shoulders shaking. "Wow, I may need to step up my game, then."

"No, no, your game is fine." She glances up at me with a grin.

"Fine? *Fine?* I'll show you fine." I gather her up in my arms and throw her over my shoulder.

"Sebastian, we can't leave our own party."

"Watch me."

The kitchen doors swing open, and if I didn't already want to punch the intruder in the face, after seeing who it is, I definitely do now.

I set Amber down gently, careful not to show her ass to my former gardener and Charlotte. I don't know why in the hell they're here, and in the grand scheme of things, I'm better off without them. I'm glad I found out the truth before I eloped with her, but I think more than anything I hate that they're in my house, which finally feels like a home again, on this special night that Amber worked her ass off for.

"Bash, how are you?" Charlotte's voice makes me clench my teeth. "This has turned out so well. I mean, it's just lovely. I can't believe what's-her-name had it in her."

"Amber." I clench my teeth, and Amber's hand squeezes my arm. "Her name is Amber, and why are you here? You weren't invited."

"No, but my daddy dearest was, and the invitation said for the whole family. Might not have been the best idea, though—a bunch of snotty brats running around. How are you supposed to focus on business?"

"It's not about business." Amber's voice is so much calmer than mine, and she's smiling pleasantly at Charlotte. "It's about connection, building real relationships with your coworkers. That's the secret to a successful working relationship. And a relationship in your personal life, as well."

Pride blooms in my chest at her comment. She's talking about us, about our relationship. Whatever status we are, it's something we're both committed to figuring out.

"Huh. And how does that work for fake relationships?" Charlotte grins wickedly at us, pulling out her phone. "Like these screenshots you sent me, Bash. About how you and Amber were just putting on a show to trick your investors, to pull the wool over my daddy's eyes. Right, Peter?"

Peter nods wordlessly at her side, a puppet on a string.

"How in the world..." And suddenly I remember where I've seen the number before. The Post-it my secretary Daniele handed me at the office recently. It must be Charlotte's new number.

"Amber, I swear I didn't send her anything." I grab Amber's hands, searching her face earnestly.

"Might be a bit too late for that." Charlotte taps her screen. "Oh, oops. They've been posted. Looks like your little trick is up, Bashy."

She turns and flounces out of the kitchen, and I hang my head, reminding myself to breathe. Sure, my business may be imploding, but right now, I'm worried about Amber. I can't lose her, and I'm afraid to look into her eyes, to see if she believes me or if Charlotte's terrible lies have poisoned us.

Our eyes meet and her hands encircle my neck. "I believe you, Bash, I promise. But I don't know how the world is going to react."

At that moment, the roar of the crowd in the next room grows and grows, the sound of everything exploding around us. "You need to get out of here. Let me deal with this."

I press two buttons on my phone and then link my arm through Amber's, leading her out the back door. Unfortunately, we didn't get a turn on the ice, and my heart hurts at the realization that our perfect night has been ruined. We turn the corner of the house, and Mike flashes his lights from the second driveway.

"I'm not leaving you, Sebastian," Amber protests, digging her heels in. "You don't need to do it alone."

"I have to protect you. I have to fix this, and I can't do the latter while trying to do the first if you're here. Please, Amber," I beg her.

Finally, she nods and gives me a soft peck on the cheek before turning wordlessly and climbing in the car. As they pull onto the road, growing smaller and smaller by the second, I glance at my phone again and am relieved that the volume is still down.

Because everything I know is going up in smoke.

TWENTY

Amber

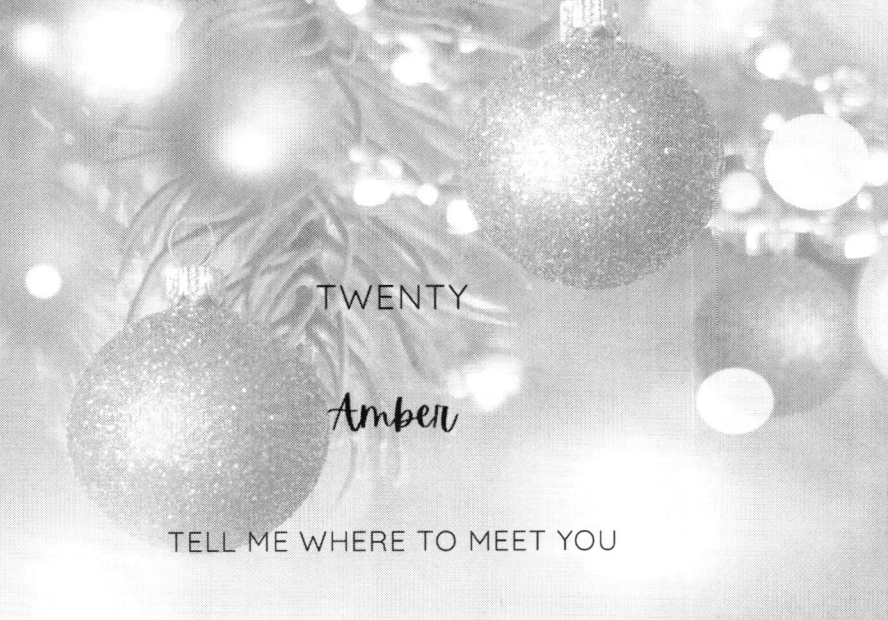

TELL ME WHERE TO MEET YOU

My mom is waiting with open arms when I arrive at her house. I called her en route so she was prepared. Mike walks me to the door despite my insistence that I can make it myself.

"You people just don't listen. Happy now?" I step over her threshold dramatically, and he nods with a chuckle.

"Mr. Sterling will be in touch, Amber." Mike's face darkens, his laugh disappearing from his eyes. "It'll all work out."

"Let's hope so." I shut the door and lock it before following my mom to her den, where she's already got our Christmas movie up and popcorn and drinks ready.

"It feels good to be doing something normal." I relax into my dad's recliner, the familiar comfort washing over me as I set my cup into the cupholder.

"I know what you mean. It's been a crazy two weeks."

"It has. A lot has happened." I pop a warm buttery piece into my mouth, savoring the flavor.

"Your father would be so proud of you. You know that, don't you?"

I shift in my seat, that old friend of mine creeping in. Self-doubt. "Would he? I took money to do all of this stuff. And I agreed to be Sebastian's fake girlfriend. That was misleading."

"Well, true. But how much of the money did you use for something selfish or something wrong?"

I can't answer, because she already knows the answer to that. The money went only to things for the party, even the servers. I never used Sebastian's credit card.

"Exactly. Okay, and sure you and Sebastian started out as something... not genuine. But look what happened."

"I'm not even sure what happened, Mom."

"Oh, don't be ridiculous. Anyone with eyes can see the two of you are crazy about each other. He looks at you as if you're made of gold. And I've never seen you so smitten over anyone."

"Well, maybe we just got caught up in the moment, in playing a part, and in the magic of the holidays."

"Ah, see that's where you're wrong. The holidays aren't magical because they're the holidays, Amber."

"Sure they are. You know how Dad always made Christmas magical."

"Exactly. Your dad made it magical. You made it magical for Sebastian, and he for you, in the end. What happened between the two of you was of your own creation, not some whim of the stars."

Her words linger in my mind long after we've watched the movie, and into the night as I'm tucked into the guest bedroom. Even if she's right, how do I know Sebastian cares? He didn't even want me there with him to deal with this.

I sit up straight in bed, his words at my departure ringing in my ears.

He never said he didn't want me there.

I grab my phone from the nightstand and swipe through it until I find the number I'm looking for.

"Hello?" Ava's wide awake, as I knew she would be. She's probably working on her damn case.

"Ava, I need your help."

"Anything. Name it."

"Well, your legal help."

"Tell me where to meet you."

TWENTY-ONE

Sebastian

I WOULDN'T HAVE IT ANY OTHER WAY

Upon Amber's request, I agreed to meet her and Ava at Sterling Enterprises the next morning. When she told me her idea, I agreed wholeheartedly. Anything to stop the insistent notifications on my phone, which I had to turn up so as not to miss anything important.

Ava's heels click on the tile of the conference room as she walks from one side of the table to the other before handing Charlotte and Peter the printout of our demands. Ava's boss, the lead lawyer from her firm, watches us curiously. I wonder what Ava had to say to convince her that this whole situation was real. It's Christmas morning, after all.

Charlotte's beady little eyes pour over the agreement and the cease and desist, and after glancing at Peter, she says, "Why should we accept this? I know you have more."

"This is a courtesy." Ava smiles at the pair, her face lacking all the warmth she usually shows. "Further action can be taken by my client. Harassment, slander, destruction of property, and theft, since you took his phone." She trails off, the list obviously a worry to Charlotte as her eyebrows disappear under her bangs.

She nods. "Fine. We accept." She grabs a pen to sign.

Ava clears her throat. "You don't want your lawyer to read over it?"

"No, it's fine." Charlotte shrugs, scrawling her name across the page as she turns to me. "So, the apartment is mine? I just have to leave you alone?"

"Please talk to me, and not my client," Ava reminds her for the millionth time. "The apartment is yours, pending you delete all social media posts about my client and make a public statement that the information wasn't the whole story. Per the agreement, you will both sign an NDA. If you ever talk about my client, tweet, post, send a letter, anything, you'll be held accountable to all punishments that apply, to the max sentence."

Charlotte pushes back from the table, crooking her finger at Peter to follow. "Fine. Whatever."

"Charlotte, wait," I call, moving to my feet. Charlotte turns on her heel, and as I walk towards her, her lips quiver. The memories of our three years together play like a movie in my mind, and I wonder if the same is happening to her. We were so happy together in the beginning, what happened? How did we become the couple at the end?

She watches me expectantly, eyes narrowed. "Yes?"

"I just—I—" Words fail me for a moment, and then the warmth beside of me, the feel of her skin on mine as her hand wraps around my fingers. I glance over and Amber smiles at me softly, and suddenly, the words aren't hiding from me anymore. I glance back at Charlotte, my confidence returned. "For a long time, I wondered what I did wrong, where we went wrong. For the first of our relationship, everything was perfect."

"It was," she agrees, her tone soft and her eyes widening, now less suspicious.

"I think I just want you to know, it wasn't you. I know I was a workaholic and I never made time for you. I see that now."

"And me cheating wasn't you, Bash." She smiles. "It was me, that was my choice. Sometimes people are meant to spend a certain amount of time together, and that's it. And they learn from it. I think that's what we were."

"A lesson," I say.

"Yes. A lesson. Good luck, both of you." Charlotte nods in farewell before disappearing through the double doors.

I finally feel like I can breathe, and when I glance at Amber, I can't help the smile that spreads across my face. She returns it, her whole face lighting up. The urge to kiss her is too strong to resist.

I lean over, covering her mouth with mine, and she kisses me back with all her might. When we break apart, she clears her throat, giving me her stern look.

"Now, next time you shoo me away instead of letting me work with you to solve a problem, I'm wrapping you up in a package."

"I wouldn't have it any other way."

"Left. Left. No, the other left, Bash," Amber dictates as we pivot the bedframe through the door. "There you go. Perfect."

We set the frame down easily on the new hardwood floors of the bedroom that remained empty for a year. My bedroom. My home. With my very real girlfriend.

"Oh god," Amber groans, collapsing to the floor.

"What? Did you hurt something?" I hurry around the bed to crouch beside her. She hasn't been seriously injured since her ankle, but she's the queen of stubbed toes and paper cuts, something I've discovered since she officially moved in with me the day after Christmas.

"No, I just realized we have to go back downstairs for the mattress." She lays her head on my shoulder. "I know we said we were gonna tackle all of our problems together, but maybe hiring movers would have been a better idea this time."

I wrap my arm around her, pulling her close to me, and lean down to whisper in her ear. "I got you a surprise, Amber."

She perks up at that, sitting up quickly. "I do like surprises."

"Oh, I know you do." Nodding toward the window, I command, "Go look outside."

She moves to her feet in the blink of an eye before skipping over to the window. She glances out, her nose pressed against the glass until it's squished.

"Sebastian Sterling, you are one of the most stubborn men I've ever met, and I'm beyond thankful for it." She sighs, and I move to my feet, coming up behind her to let her rest against me. We both look down at the movers that just arrived. They hop out of the second truck and gather around the first so they can lift our new mattress out as a team.

"Thankful, huh?"

"Yes, very thankful." She wiggles her ass against my groin, and I growl in her ear.

"We have to behave until the movers leave."

"How else can I show my thanks, then?" She turns in my arms, her lips pursed in a sexy pout.

"It is New Year's. Why don't you celebrate with me by making a resolution?" It's sensitive territory. I know how she feels about the holiday, but I'm banking on the fact that we're both making changes in our lives, and I'm hoping life doesn't scare her as much anymore.

"My resolution is to start my own party planning business," she finally replies and smiles up at me. She's mentioned it in passing, but hearing her say it as a resolution makes my heart swell with pride. "Your turn, Mr. Sterling."

"My resolution is to keep being the best sugar papa I can," I joke, and she swats at me playfully before reaching up to kiss me enthusiastically. Amber didn't just make me enjoy the holidays again, she reignited my love for life, and I can't wait to live mine with her.

Sebastian

EPILOGUE
THE NEXT CHRISTMAS

Home. I'm home. After cutting the engine of my car, I take a moment to just admire my home. It's no longer the house or the estate to me; now it genuinely feels like a safe place, and while Amber has helped make that happen, I also like to think I made some progress myself. It's been almost a year since she moved in with me permanently. It's been an amazing year of love and laughter, but we've also had our moments. What couple doesn't? I've learned not to leave my wet shoes in the foyer because she despises stepping in puddles with her wet socks. And while I'm no doubt a gem to live with, Amber did agree to my request to not rearrange the whole damn kitchen. I know where everything is and I like it that way, and I cook more than she does.

After testing one another's boundaries and limits we found our groove and our lives have fallen into a routine. Amber started her own event planning services and is in the process of opening her own venue, as well. She also helps Sterling Enterprises occasionally. Hey, when your girlfriend is a superhero at planning shit, sometimes you have to call in a favor. A cloud moves over the sun, darkening the sky a bit, and I glance at my watch to double-check the time. It's later than I realized, and I hurry out of the car and around to the passenger side. I scoop up the basket with Amber's Christmas present and lock up the car, cradling the basket in both hands as I make my way up the front steps and into the house. Thankfully, the weather's clear and my shoes are safe to leave in the foyer.

The house is silent but comforting, candles lit around the living room, and the fireplace roaring and warm. The presents are now under the tree and from the looks of it, Amber has filled my stocking. I filled hers already, and I've had to keep her from peeking all week. It would have ruined the surprise that I got her. I slip the basket under the tree, hiding it behind a bigger box. Gizmo greets me first, the bells of his sweater jingling all the way as he sniffs around Amber's present. "Hey, quit being nosy." He narrows his eyes at me but obeys, following me to the couch. The doors from the kitchen burst open, revealing the beautiful, hilarious, and... spirited leading lady of my life. Our eyes lock and my breath catches in my throat. She's absolutely beautiful, even if she's in an ugly Christmas sweater. She asked me to pick a theme for the evening and, to my surprise, she had snarled her nose at it.

Apparently, Amber doesn't like one thing about Christmas.

But here she is in a swamp green fluffy sweater peppered with pompom balls and mismatched pajama pants. And I don't think I've ever seen anything or anyone lovelier in all my life.

I reach for her hand, but she walks right by me, grabbing our stockings and then returning to sit by me.

"Don't you want to wait for everyone else?" I ask, knowing that our friends and family will be here in a bit, all dressed in ugly sweaters, as well.

"No, I'm too excited to wait." She claps her hands together. "I'll even let you go first, though." Her face splits into a grin, her joy infectious until my own face hurts from smiling.

"No, no, you go first this time." It's good timing, really. I'd hate for her surprise to be ruined by waiting. It's a time sensitive matter.

"Okay okay, you talked me into it." She squeals, her hand diving into the opening of her stocking. Her lips purse in concentration as she feels around, as if she's guessing at what's in there.

Finally, she pulls out a piece of paper, and as her eyes follow the words, my excitement builds. Higher and higher until I think I might explode before her eyes meet mine. Her mouth drops in an O, no sound coming out, and suddenly, I'm unsure of my surprise. Maybe it's not something she would want, after all. She flashes the paper around, displaying the text to me.

"How did you know?"

Amber

"How did I know? I was there, Amber." He laughs. "I handpicked her for you." He reaches for his stocking.

My heart catches in my throat, emotion filling my eyes and I wordlessly hand it over. "I guess you don't need to open this, then."

He gives me an odd look before reaching inside, grasping

around as I did. He pulls out the small rectangle, glancing at me then down at the image, then back at me again. "Wait. Amber. This isn't what I got you."

I burst out laughing, unable to stop the giggles from spilling between my lips. The paper that he left in my stocking with the words "Our family is growing" slips from between my fingers and a noise from under the tree alerts us both, and Gizmo. He jumps off the arm of the couch, stalking towards the gifts, and, to my surprise, a figure emerges from the presents, stretching its little legs and then letting out a big yawn.

The puppy's eyes focus on us then, her face erupting into the characteristic grin of a pit bull. She bounds over to the couch, and I bend over to pick her up.

"Easy, easy," Sebastian warns.

"Oh, I'm fine. I'm pregnant, not helpless." I shush him, cuddling my new furry friend. She settles into my lap immediately, her head pressed against my stomach.

"Thought of a name?" The puppy glances up at me as if she knows I'm talking about her.

"I'm still digesting the news," Sebastian replies, tracing the outline of our baby's face. "Now I'm kind of mad at you, Angel."

"Why?" I sit up straighter, startling the bundle of fur in my lap.

"There's no way I can top this gift, ever." He sets the picture and stockings on the empty cushion beside of him before moving as close to me as he can get and taking my face in his hands. He stares into my eyes, and I marvel at the love and devotion seeping from him, surrounding me in a safe, warm haven. He presses his lips to mine, and I reciprocate, kissing him with my whole heart.

When we pull apart, Gizmo jumps up into Sebastian's lap

and I glance over to see Willow slinking along the back of the couch, settling in behind us and her tail flicking my shoulder. Our family has grown by six more legs. I can't wait to see what our future, our happily ever after, holds.

AUTHOR'S NOTE

Wow. This book was a blast for me, and that's saying something after a few tough years of writer's block. Thank you for taking a chance on Bash and Amber's story. I hope you enjoyed their romance as much as I did! If you'd like to keep up with my future books, you can join my FB group here-My FB Group

And sign up for my newsletter here -Sign up for my newsletter Holiday Hotties Book Two will release in January 2023! Ava is getting her own book!

Rock Star Cupid Coming January 2023. Preorder now- Preorder Rockstar Cupid

ALSO BY K LEIGH

Holiday Hotties

Rockstar Cupid (Ava's Story)

Sparks with the Single Dad (Phoebe's Story)

My Ex, the Pumpkin King (Rachel's Story)

Life Unfiltered Series

Undeveloped

The Robinson Sisters Series

Four Day Prince Charming

One Week Queen

Standalone Novels

Twist of Fate

Poetry

My Burning Depths Series

Wait on Me, Okay?

I'll Be Here

Nows

Made in the USA
Columbia, SC
28 July 2024